THORN

THOrN

Betty Levin

*For Maggie,
good friend, good
writer. What more
might we ask for?
With love,
Betty*

Front Street
ASHEVILLE, NORTH CAROLINA

Library of Congress Cataloging-in-Publication Data
Levin, Betty.
Thorn / Betty Levin. – 1st ed.
p. cm.
Summary: Thorn, a mysterious boy with a deformed leg, arrives on
an island inhabited by the people of the Singing Seals, and though treated
with fear and suspicion by most of the natives, is befriended by the girl
Willow, chosen to be the next Keeper of Story.
ISBN 1-932425-46-2 (alk. paper)
[1. Islands–Fiction.2. Friendship–Fiction.3. Fantasy.] I. Title.
PZ7.L5783Tm 2005
[Fic]–dc22
2005012682

Front Street
An Imprint of Boyds Mills Press, Inc.
A Highlights Company

For Caroline and Alvin
and for Melle
in memory of their Grandpa John

THORN

The men want to turn back. They fear they will never again stand on solid ground. The journey has been longer than they expected. Longer because the winds have blown against us. Because none of us had ever left our own island before now. Because my father insists that we keep heading toward the dawn whether or not it is break of day.

My father studies the knucklebone with marks on it that his father gave him long ago. He gazes at the night sky, then again at the bone. He points. He tells two men to row, just that one side. Then he lets out rope, and the boat turns and dips. The men cling to the edge in terror. They still expect that the boat will take to its wing and carry them into the sky. They fear the sky even more than they fear these waves.

What do I fear? Being left among strangers who speak a different way. Still, I think that fear will not overwhelm me, for it is not so wounding as the greater fear I strive to banish by giving it no name.

Our food is gone. We have little left to drink. The icy sea splashes over us but leaves our skin burning, and we are crusted and cracked from the salt.

The men want to turn back. They do not trust my father and his winged craft. Yet they still hope that if I am given to the people of my father's father and mother, there will be healing on the High Island. I am their offering.

When my father built this boat, he let me help him. The

men do not think I can work that way, but my father knows which tasks he can put me to. So he taught me just as his father taught him, and then we practiced together. Sometimes he let me hold the rope or the steering oar. I doubt that I could do as much now, for I grow weak when I do not use my walking leg. I dread the long struggle ahead to regain my strength.

Father says that when I am on solid ground again, my walking leg will bear me up as before. Meanwhile, he tells me to stay active in other ways. I should sharpen my wits, he says. When I ask how, he smiles and suggests I apply my fire stone. The fire stone will sharpen almost anything. Sometimes my father is playful even when he means what he says.

Before we left the High Island he told me that all that mattered to him was saving me. That is why he encouraged the men in their belief that if they gave me back to his father's and mother's people, their ailing children would grow strong.

Even so, I can tell that the men are tempted to throw me into the sea and be done with this misery. They want to turn back.

I would join my sister then. My father said she was too small to know what was done to her. She feared nothing. She felt nothing. But it would be terrible for me, he said.

This is the fear I have kept from my thoughts. Now, though, it rushes at me like the waves themselves. What I would banish overwhelms me, and once again I am in the first boat my father and his father made. I am there when it flips over. I cannot forget the helpless plunge, the cold that seized me, the seawater that I gulped and gulped until my head would burst. I do not recall my father saving me, although

I know that he did. Still, I can almost taste the burning that gripped me in the days that followed, and I know that I fear the sea more than anything else.

My father built this boat to spare me. He explained to the men what this journey could accomplish. Even now he shows a confidence he may not feel, but the men feel it and so do I. So we go on. Dawn after dawn.

When at last we spy land, we may change course to follow the coast until we come to a stack. My father's father and mother said that the stack is like a single rugged rock as tall as the High Island. Father thinks he will recognize it when we come upon it, even though he has never before set eyes on it.

The men despair. This ordeal has driven the desired outcome from their thoughts. By now, all that keeps them from casting me from the boat is my father, who would abandon them if they did. They know he would come after me into the sea. Without him and his marked bone, this boat would flounder like a wounded bird, a prey to the hungry waves. They would be lost.

WILLOW

Willow was spreading out strips of fish to dry when Crab and Thistle came racing down from the headland. Resentful at being kept from all their doings, she tried to ignore the alarm they raised. But everyone else looked up and listened. The boys were yelling and running so hard they could barely be understood.

"Boat!" croaked Thistle.

"A winged boat!" gasped Crab.

The men glanced out to sea. Might the boys have glimpsed a creature from afar, like the great-toothed seal? Did it fly or swim?

The boys stuck to their sighting.

"A boat! It was a boat," insisted Thistle.

"There are men within," added Crab. "One standing up called out. He asked if we were the People of the Singing Seals."

"Say more about the wings," ordered old Gray Cloud, swatting Thistle across the head. "You have told us nothing."

Thistle reeled but managed to keep his footing.

Willow's father said, "You should have called us to you so that we could see with our own eyes."

Crab said feebly, "We ran as fast as ever we could all the way from the cliff."

"Go back, then," ordered Uncle Redstone. "Keep watch."

"We have been there since dawn," Thistle said, sounding dejected.

No one but Willow seemed to realize what he was trying

to say. But she knew at once that the boys, her friends, had been without food the day long. She slipped away to her hut, where she dug a piece of fish from the embers and stuffed it into her pouch.

Outside she chose the long way around, behind the inland mound of shells and bones that banked the cluster of huts. She forced herself not to run, since that would likely draw attention. If any of the women caught her leaving, they would bring her back and set her to work again.

As the ground rose, she caught sight of the boys on the shoulder of the hill. She quickened her pace until they were within earshot. Then she called to them. She ran the remaining distance and thrust her pouch into their hands. They tore at the fish, cramming it into their mouths.

As soon as they were on their way again, she started back. From this higher ground she could see thin plumes of smoke rising and hovering over the settlement. She cast her eyes past the haze to the familiar dunes and beyond them to the beach. The sea flicked harmless waves landward, tiny tongues seeking a taste of sun-warmed sand.

Farther out, larger, gentle swells slapped against the outlying rocks and wreathed the base of the great stack with foam. Seabirds, shrill and reckless in their hunting frenzy, glinted as they swooped over the water. And something else! Something else out there! A boat gliding around the headland. It bobbed and dipped like a thing alive. Its single wing cast a flint-sharp shadow that seemed to slice the water's surface as if to part it from the depths.

Willow pelted downhill and into the midst of her people. "The boat!" she cried. "With a wing! Coming here!" She pointed toward the headland.

Now everyone rushed to the shore. But from the lower ground the boat was not yet visible. The men began to turn away, Uncle Redstone muttering about the light or maybe the children playing tricks on the elders.

"Father," Willow implored, "I truly saw it." But he ignored her, as he usually did when he was with the uncles.

Not for the first time she wondered why she couldn't be Crab or Thistle. Until this greening season, Willow had outclimbed the boys on the rocky stack and hunted with them along the ledges and clung to a long tree-boat, even when it was slammed and tumbled by breaking waves. Then the women had taken her in hand to teach her the skills of her kind.

In this settlement, unflawed girls were so rare that long before they were grown they were watched and raised up to become mothers. Even Great Mother, who had chosen Willow to be the next Keeper of Story, agreed that she must quit the rigors and perils of boy deeds.

"Let Hazel be a mother," Willow had argued. "She wants to be."

"Hazel is not enough. Hazel and Willow are not enough." Great Mother had sounded impatient. Maybe she was doubting her decision to rely on Willow. These days Great Mother seemed increasingly irritable.

Where was Great Mother now? Trudging off alone somewhere, Willow supposed. Seeking, she would tell Willow, who plied her with questions about those frequent absences.

What she was seeking, Great Mother never said. These days her eyes seemed so filmed that Willow wondered how Great Mother would recognize what she sought even if she stumbled over it.

Willow retreated to the settlement and took herself behind the work place to where the shell heap placed her within reach of the roof. Clambering up, she groped for the great whalebone that supported the sealskins spanning the walls of the work place. Not for the first time, she flattened herself and crept forward until she could feel the ridge of bone beneath her. Now she paused and raised her head.

She had a good view of the disgruntled men as they grouped and regrouped, waiting in uneasy anticipation for a winged boat to appear. If there were such a boat, the doubters would be saying.

Willow propped her chin in her hands and peered out toward the headland. She would observe the boat as it headed for the beach. She would be the first to see what manner of men it brought.

Was it a true boat? How could it be? Boats were made from trees that grew far away in the valley. This vessel was entirely different, and not only because of its wing, which was flapping now as if broken. Rather than being long like the trunk of a tree, this craft was shaped like an enormous egg or basket.

But what basket could hold four men—no, five—without sinking?

Willow shaded her eyes with both hands as she gazed out over the dazzling water. Yet another, smaller head appeared over the side of the strange boat as it slid from wave to trough. One man stood up to reach the wing. He dragged it down until it collapsed in a heap. A piece of it remained upright, a staff as slender as a young tree or a long, straight bone.

Two men raised oars and stroked the water. As the boat

moved landward, Willow slithered off her roof perch and ran across the dunes to the beach.

The man standing at the staff was clothed in a strange gray garment roped in at the waist. Otherwise he looked like one of the people on the shore. "I bring you my son, Thorn," he called to them. "Care for him as if he were your own, for he is, partly."

Someone shouted back to him, "You are mistaken. You do not speak like one of us. We hear your words, but the sound is not ours."

"I was born and raised among the people of the High Island," the man explained. "A long time ago my father and mother were rescued by voyagers from afar who happened upon them clinging to a rock. They were brought to the High Island, where they learned its ways. But they kept their own speech as well, so I grew up learning it and long afterward was able to teach it to my son. He is accustomed to the language of the High Island, but I have taught him your words. In time he will adopt the sounds of them."

"If your father came from us, why did he not return here?" an uncle demanded.

"He tried," the man told them. "When the rescuers left my mother and father on the rocky shore of the High Island, they filled their pouches with birds and departed. My father attempted to make a boat like the craft that plucked him and my mother from the sea, but it was not seaworthy. This boat," the man continued, "is fashioned after it, according to recollection."

"So the High Island kept your mother and father," Uncle Redstone concluded.

"And keeps me yet," the man replied. "When the winged

boat carried a man and woman to live among them, it visited sickness upon the island as well. But I was born strong and soon became skilled at climbing the bird cliffs. I provided more than one man's share of birds and eggs for the High Island. In time an island woman joined me, and I came to regard myself as one of her people. Then she gave birth to twins, which cannot be raised. The people of the High Island believed this wrong birth to be a sign that a man from away was not meant to join with one of their women."

The gathering on the beach turned inward. Although Willow couldn't hear what was said, she caught the taut, frantic gestures of alarm.

"Hear me," the man in the boat pleaded. "Believe me. Take my son. He will bring good fortune to you."

Willow's father stepped forward. After glancing back at the others, he called out, partly in warning, partly in protest, "We have troubles enough. We want no sickness here."

The man in the boat said, "My son survived. He thrives. You will see all he can do. From his birth, when his twin was given to the sea, he grew straight and strong. He would prove as skilled on the bird cliffs as I. Then the sickness returned. It seized my son and his mother, killing her, maiming him. He bears its sign as a wound carries its scar. That is all."

Once again the people on the beach spoke among themselves. All the while they glanced uneasily at the boat swirling in eddies as the rowers sought to steady it.

Another uncle stepped into the shallows. "We do not know of any man and woman stranded on a rock," he declared. "Your son would be a stranger here. You should keep him."

"They will not have him," the man replied. "When the sickness returned and lodged in him, they thought to cast him adrift or to offer him, like his twin, to the sea. Then they deemed it more fitting to give him back to those from whom we came. So I pieced this craft according to my father's and mother's recollection of the rescue boat, and I reversed, as best I could, the course that brought them to the High Island, which from here lies farther than far in the path of the setting sun."

"Why not stay here with him?" asked Gray Cloud.

"These men would not find their way home without me," the man replied. "Besides, as long as I am able to gather birds and eggs from the cliffs, they have need of me."

One of the rowers lurched to his feet, upsetting the vessel's balance. He wore a similar garment, but he was shorter and his hair was dark. As he staggered, the boat dipped and took the backsplash of a wave. This made him lose his footing and unleash a torrent of furious but unfamiliar words.

The people on the shore drew into a knot.

The man at whom the anger was hurled held fast to the upright staff. "These men dare not tarry," he called to the people on the beach. "They have scant liking for this craft and even less for me. They hear us speak and cannot understand what we say. So they fear I will abandon them to stay with my son. They will not allow the boat to land."

Even as he spoke, two of the rowers reached for rockweed floating close by but rooted to a boulder. They pulled the boat against it. Another rower lifted the boy up and over the side. As the boat lurched back, the boy fell on the slippery weed. Flailing as the water rose around him, he grabbed first one fistful of rockweed and then another until he could haul himself onto the boulder. There he clung, drenched and shivering.

Willow stared and stared. There was something jarring about the boy. But his instant aloft had been so brief that it was like glimpsing a fin that surfaces and sinks all at the same time. Was she simply distracted by his strange garment, like that of his father and the rowers? Now tangled, it clung to him, concealing more than it revealed. Or maybe it was his black hair and slight stature that gave him such an arresting look.

Before the oarsmen could take their places to paddle into deeper water, the boy's father leaned down, scooped up a pouch from the bottom of the boat, and hurled it over their heads. Reaching for it, the boy lost his grip on the rockweed and slipped once more. An uncle ran to launch a tree-boat. Meanwhile the boy floundered, hindered by the pouch he clasped while trying to regain the boulder.

The uncle shoved the tree-boat into the shallows and paddled out to the boy. Even when it bumped alongside the rock and the uncle extended an oar to the boy, Willow wasn't sure of what she had so briefly glimpsed.

But when the boy stepped ashore, leaning on the oar for support, she did see. Everyone did.

He swiveled on one leg, turning to look out at the departing boat, its wing already half raised and fluttering wildly in a freshening breeze.

He was the only person on the beach watching his father struggle to raise the wing to its full height. Everyone else stood transfixed, gaping at the boy's thin, crooked leg, at the useless foot that dangled, toes down, barely touching the ground.

At once he was surrounded. Willow didn't get another look until everyone started across the dunes toward the settlement. As Uncle Redstone, carrying the boy, strode briskly ahead, she caught one sidelong glance of the crooked leg.

Was it a leg? It looked so white and thin that it gave the impression of bare bone with possibly a trace of skin. The thought sent a shudder through her.

When Uncle Redstone reached the entry passage to the huts, he set the boy down. Without the oar to lean on, the boy's body twisted sideways. Every halting step dragged.

Willow was shoved back by elders crowding the entry. As whispered reports were sent along the curving passage, she learned that the boy was warming by the hearth in the hut shared by her uncle Redstone and Bramble and Willow and her father. So she waited until the first crush of people had satisfied their curiosity. She could still savor the excitement that had transformed this ordinary greening time into a notable event.

She reveled in every rare happening, like the beaching of a whale or the sighting of an immense tree afloat on the current. A tree meant precious wood to be shared for building and tools. A whale provided meat and oil and bone. It wasn't only that most daily tasks were set aside at such times, but that the rhythm of the settlement was altered. And it usually ended with a feast.

But was this boy's arrival a cause for celebration? He brought nothing useful, was himself the gift, and a sorry one at that. Meanwhile the giver was flying across the water, on his way to the High Island, a place that no one had ever heard of before, let alone seen.

By the time Willow was able to enter the hut, the boy, now clothed in a sealskin garment, was holding out his hands to the smoldering fire. Except for his crooked leg, he looked more like other boys his size.

Willow sidled up to him for a closer look. The leg, for all

it was worth, might as well have been bone. Yet there was visible flesh covered by skin as white as the belly of a fish. The foot wasn't so much misshapen as shrunken and almost blue with cold. She stooped to feel it but was yanked back by one of the uncles.

"Is there pain in it?" she asked.

The uncle told her touching the boy might harm her. Like fire, he added.

She asked the boy, "Is there fire in your leg?"

He said, "No. Ice."

She reached for dried seaweed to place upon the embers. Her uncle didn't stop her, so she blew on the ashes to start a new flame.

"Are you hungry?" she asked him.

"They fed me," he said. "I thirst."

Everyone in the hut was speaking in undertones. She caught bits of the discussion, attempts at identifying the boy's father, questions about the High Island. Was it the Last Island, where the Boundless dwell and where hunters sometimes land when they are swept out to sea?

Willow brought the boy a bowl of nettle broth and set it beside him. He drank it down all at once, started to hand back the empty bowl, then shoved it across the flagstone at her instead. He drew himself closer to the small flame, which was already subsiding into the ashes. He looked around, first at the bed closets in the walls, then at the layers of flat stones that spanned the wall across from the doorway. "It is very dark. Do all of you keep in the ground like this?" he asked Willow.

"This is a hut, a living-place," she replied, puzzled. If his father's father came from here, he should know how her people lived. *His* people, partly.

Behind them voices were raised in disagreement. One of the uncles and his woman argued that the boy should be returned to the sea. Willow's father objected. They should be mindful of what the sea had long ago taken from the People of the Singing Seals. Great Mother, who had been a child when the sea had risen in a monstrous wave, breaking over the land and the living, still spoke of it with horror. If the mother and father of this boy's father had somehow survived the Wave, the boy should be kept and sheltered and fed, lest the sea, enraged, devour the next of their own to be caught in a storm.

"But we are not certain he is a child of the Wave," warned the uncle.

"Or of the Last Island," added another.

"Then we must wait for a sign," Willow's father told them.

"His leg is a sign," said the uncle. "That and his empty belly and open mouth."

"No doubt there are tasks within his reach." Willow's father turned to the boy. "What skills do you bring?" he asked.

"Nets and baskets," the boy answered. "I helped my father craft the boat that carried us all this way. Also," he added, "beasts come to me. Some stay." He faltered. "And some leave their shadows with me. So I make their shadow shapes as I am able."

Willow's father scowled. "Enough!"

The boy sensed his displeasure without understanding it. "I make fair shadow beasts," he offered.

"You have said enough if you are to remain among us, at least for now."

"Remain?" demanded Uncle Redstone, his gaze sweeping the hut and resting on one bed closet and then another. "And sleep here? With us?"

The men and women regarded the boy. Then Bramble shook her head. "He must not be touched until we know that those who bore him here are not tainted with his crookedness. He can sleep outside or in the work place."

They all went out, leaving Thorn beside the hearth. Willow remained with him. She said, "The work place is nearby."

Thorn shrugged as if to say that it was all the same to him, work place or bed closet.

"I will bring you skins for warmth," she told him.

He didn't reply.

She pointed to the bed closets in the thick walls. "There my father sleeps, there my uncle Redstone and his woman, who is Bramble, and their Little Gray Bird. Here behind the jars is where you empty yourself; it goes under the floor and out. And when you are ready, I will take you to the stream that brings us water."

"Where is my tunic?" he asked. "Where is my pouch?"

She found the pouch in her father's bed closet. She didn't know what the boy meant by "tunic," but she saw nothing else that might belong to him. She squatted down to watch, curious to see what he would take from the pouch. He started to open it, then changed his mind. And so they stayed that way, he clutching the pouch to himself, she waiting sharp-eyed and eager, like a bird stalking a cricket.

THORN

They dwell in darkness. All is stone and the reek of things left to spoil. Father said they are my true people, or partly so. He said this is my true home, or partly so. But I have known only the High Island, where we live in air and wind and light.

They fear that I bring the taint of crookedness. It pains them to look upon my leg. Yet they cannot shift their eyes from it. And such eyes! Sharp as flung stones, those eyes, pale as the sky in the thaw time, some nearly hidden by falls of hair as white as bleached grains.

I do not know what they have done with my tunic, and I have seen no garment here like it. They wear the skins of beasts, heavy garments, yet warming to a body chilled by the earth's dank breath. Before I was put out of the boat, I noticed sheep on the outlying rocks. They do not look like those we keep on the High Island that graze on the inland meadows. The sheep here are smaller. They seem to feed on rockweed or kelp.

The people will not have me in their sleeping hut. I am to stay where they work. It has more space and even some light that filters down through roof skins. It is full of flint chips and bones and even bits of wood, though empty of people. The girl, Willow, who brings me water and food, says that in this greening season most work is done in the sunlight. I suppose I may be sent outside when they decide to return here.

For now, though, no one comes, not even the dog I glimpsed through the doorway. It glanced my way and then skulked off. It is the only dog I have seen so close to the huts and the only dog I have known to shun me.

Maybe all will be different here. Maybe the beasts of this land will be wary of me. It troubles me that this place is so different from all my father told me to expect. If these are not his father's and mother's people, my father will never know.

WILLOW

As usual, Willow strayed from the others. It wasn't exactly deliberate. Ever since she had been separated from Crab and Thistle for their daily tasks, it just seemed to happen time and again. At the last greening season she and the boys had still been together, always joined in common effort when they weren't testing one another. Now, on this bright day when they might have been racing to the hill's summit, she didn't even know what the boys were doing.

It wasn't until she had to lay aside her bundle of roots and stems and start digging and collecting a new bunch that she noticed the distance she had covered over the windswept heath. Here on this hillside she was alone with the meadow birds and the swiftly changing clouds.

She paused, scanning the sweep of land for roving dogs. When she saw there was no clear danger, she took a moment to gaze at the undulating grasses. Sometimes after a storm the sea looked like this, great mounds of water heaving and subsiding and heaving again. Here, away from the shore, the rise and fall of waving green seemed to possess a rhythm of its own. She planted her feet apart in response to that seeming motion, but the land did not rock her as the sea would have done.

She dropped her digging bone beside the bundle, glanced quickly about, and raced with outstretched arms to the summit of the hill. There she paused. The far side descended to a marsh where the uncles sometimes hunted ducks. But it was an area that caused uneasiness among the people. This was due to the nearby stones they occasionally quarried, good flat building stones, but hauntingly regular, giving people the impression that they might be pillaging their ancestors' burial ground.

Willow turned to face the way she had come. Sinking to her knees, she made herself into a tree-boat. Her hand became an oar that shoved her free, and then she rolled just as she used to do when she was little. Over and over she went, her eyes tightly shut, so that she saw nothing, heard nothing, while feeling only the headlong rush.

When she finally stopped, she allowed herself a lingering moment of dizziness before opening her eyes to the bright day.

Only it wasn't entirely bright, because something dark loomed above her. Not something, but someone. Willow squinted up at the figure, and all at once exhilaration drained from her, for she recognized the gaunt frame and severe face of Great Mother. The old woman's silence goaded Willow into action. She stumbled to her feet. For a confused instant she couldn't locate her bundle of roots and stems. Then she recalled that it was halfway up the hill. So was her digging bone.

"And if a hungry dog had come upon you," said Great Mother, sounding as if she were continuing a speech already delivered, "what a tender morsel for her pups you would make."

In the past when Great Mother spoke harsh words, sometimes her eyes would hold a sparkle of laughter. Then Willow knew that if you caused no further mischief, Great Mother might turn away with a chuckle, and the encounter would be over. But now the sparkle was gone. Willow could feel Great Mother's displeasure, heavy and hard as stone.

Willow mumbled, "You go off for days by yourself and are not eaten."

"One day I may fall prey to a hungry beast, but not as long as hares and burrowing creatures abound. The dog that chews through this tough skin would spit me out and leave my bones for the crows to finish. But you, Willow, are a ready meal. You have been kept and fed and taught your crafts to prepare you for motherhood, as well as to be the next Keeper of Story. The People of the Singing Seals have need of you, and I have not chosen you to take my place only to have you squander such knowledge by becoming some wild beast's next meal. Do you hear me, Willow? Your life is not to be risked."

"I hear you, Great Mother," Willow replied.

"How many bundles have you gathered today?" Great Mother asked her.

"Just one," Willow said. "But so much has happened since you went away. The days are different now."

The old woman said grimly, "No days are entirely alike. This I can assure you, for I have seen many."

Willow wanted to ask her whether she had found what she was seeking, but the look of weariness in Great Mother's pale eyes did not invite questions. Willow started to tell her about the winged boat and the boy with the crooked leg, but Great Mother was already dismissing her.

"Collect your roots and digger," the old woman ordered. "Follow me until you can rejoin the others. Then see that you do your share."

Willow trudged up the hill to retrieve her bundle and digging bone. Then she had to run after Great Mother, who had walked off without looking back.

Almost as soon as Willow caught sight of the others kneeling and bending among the weeds, Great Mother gave a curt nod in their direction. Quick to obey, Willow dashed over to join them. They took no more notice of her arrival than they had of her departure.

Willow suspected that Great Mother saw their unknowing. Still, she continued on her way without pause or comment, without even a word of greeting.

In this greening season, not only was night slow to descend, but it barely held its own against the strident thrust of morning. So a day's work often seemed unending.

To ease the strain on their backs and shoulders, the women brought their bundles to a communal pile where the few young children watched over the only infant in their midst. During the break from the stooping and digging and cutting, the women stayed and chatted while Sorrel nursed her baby. The other children, set free for a spell, went running and leaping like lambs at dusk. The older girls, Willow and Hazel, were too tired to play but too young to speak out as women.

Still, Willow listened to the talk. Only one thing preyed on their minds: Thorn, the boy with the shrunken leg. First and foremost there was the danger to Mizzle's unborn child. If the boy cast his eyes upon Mizzle, would his look maim the infant she carried? And what of the little boys, who had survived the hazards of early life so far? With so few growing to adulthood, every one of them was precious. Even the infant, who had no fingers, was nurtured in the hope that they might yet grow from his hands.

Tall Reed reminded the other women that the boy's father had said that his son would bring good fortune. "The boy himself survived. Might he not cast enduring strength instead of sickness and weakness into the little ones?"

"Until we have seen his leg repair," Diving Bird retorted, "it is best not to risk the outcome."

As others spoke up, her position prevailed. Yet agreement did nothing to dispel their curiosity about the winged boat, its spokesman, and the boy. They were still muttering to themselves as they resumed their digging and cutting and gathering.

When the afternoon wore into evening, Tall Reed signaled the end of the day's work. Sealskins were unrolled, the bundled roots stacked on them for dragging home.

Willow and Hazel joined forces. The flippers on the skin they hauled were pierced so that they could drive their digging bones through the holes to become grab bars. Tired though they were, they couldn't resist hurrying as they neared the settlement. As the laden sealskin bounced and swerved over the ground, bundled roots were flung off. The girls ran on, ignoring Tall Reed's shouts.

But the girls were sent back. There would be no eating until all the bundles left behind had been retrieved.

Even after this task was completed, all they would get was the last of the fish, mostly bone and scaly skin. Of course they must thrive and grow strong, Tall Reed said to them, but a missed meal would do no harm, and it might teach them to waste nothing. Her scowl was directed at Willow, who tended to lead Hazel astray.

Hopeful that she might yet find food, Willow entered the crowded hut. But when Great Mother glanced her way, Willow retreated to the back wall. There she waited, inhaling the smoky aroma of the meal but too far from the hearth to snatch up the food scraps that slipped between the uncles' fingers and fell to the littered floor.

She half listened to Great Mother's questions about the winged boat and the man who claimed to be one of them, even though his birth took place on a distant island.

"What names did he give for his father and mother?" Great Mother asked.

The men and women exchanged looks in the flickering dimness.

Great Mother uttered a grunt of disgust. "Did no one here insist that he account for himself?"

"It ended of a sudden," said one uncle.

"When the boy was left, we made haste to bring him out of the sea," said another.

"Only one man spoke," Willow's father told Great Mother. "He said his father's mother and father had been plucked from a rock in the sea."

Great Mother bobbed slowly on her pad of skins. Finally she asked, "From the Wave? Did you demand to know if they were left by the Wave that flooded the land?"

Willow's father said, "There was no time to question."

Great Mother shook her head. "When the sea came, I was only a young child. There were many hut clusters then, many people. We had driven the sheep to the valley of trees, to bear their lambs and start new lives on grass and buds and leaves. The men led the way home with trees and deer. Most of the women went ahead with them. I carried one of the babies. I was with those who lagged behind because of the little ones."

"Could the man and woman rescued from a rock have been two of those who went ahead?" asked Willow's father.

Great Mother shook her head. "It does not seem likely, when I recall what we found, or did not find. We heard the roar, the terrible roar that was the Wave, but we never saw it. By the time we drew near, everything was seawater and—" She broke off, covering her eyes with her hands as though to block the sight.

After a moment she spoke again. "You have heard me tell this before. You know about the parts of huts and tree-boats and deer and dogs and people all afloat. You know about the sand that seeped into everything when the sea drew back, and the ash that fell from the sky."

"Were any boats or people recovered?" asked Uncle Redstone.

"Many bodies, yes. Only scraps of boats. We were confined to the land, and the land was all but spoiled from seawater. Afterward great trees were sighted, torn from some distant forest. We could see huge roots rear up like antlers of deer the size of whales. But our people had no boats with which to capture those trees. No one knew where they came from or where they went. Then at the next greening time two such trees were washed ashore beyond the headland. They were used, every bit of them."

"Should the boy be given back to the sea?" Willow's father asked.

"It is too soon to decide. We must learn more about him and the High Island that sheltered his father's mother and father. If it is the Last Island, then he must be Boundless. But as of now we do not know enough about it, so we cannot yet tell whether he might restore our vigor or threaten our livelihood. Or he could be as worthless as a wounded bird that flaps upon the sand, barely a morsel for man or dog."

The boy! Was he hungry by now? Willow edged along the wall past her father's bed closet until she reached the passage. Silently she made her way through the darkness, her fingers following the curve of the wall, her feet familiar with every stone she trod. She had to go out to enter the work place.

With the dark night sky above the roof, it was futile to seek him out, so she whispered, "Where are you?"

"Here," came a reply from a corner.

"She will question you," Willow told him.

"They already did," he said.

"No, it will be Great Mother, who remembers. She knows everything."

Thorn did not reply.

Willow said, "Did they feed you?"

"Yes. More than I could eat."

"If you have it still," Willow said, approaching the dark corner, "I will take it away, lest the stinky birds steal it and cover you with slime." Crouching, she reached out. Her groping fingers found his thin leg. Smothering a cry, she recoiled.

Thorn shoved something in her direction. She could smell the fish. Cautiously she touched it, then scooped it up and backed away from him.

"I have no water," he said.

"I can bring you some," she replied, ready to turn and run from the work place. She would do as she promised. But first she would deal with the remains of his fish. She scrambled around to the rear of the shell heap and squatted down to feast on the smoky meat, spitting the tiny bones around to her side until all that remained was the taste on her fingers. These she licked until nothing was left, not even the smell.

THORN

No one stopped me when I ventured from the work place. The elders turned their faces from me. But the youngest children, who all seem to be boys, closed in around me, staring, until a woman called them off.

Now as I make my way to the shore, young and old step aside in haste as if I were huge as a whale or fearsome to behold.

Before I left the work place, an old, old woman spoke to me. She wanted to know about the High Island. I could not tell her what she was trying to unearth. "It is rocky and high," I said, "with treacherous ledges all around and meadowland on top. Our houses are made of turf, and they are not connected like these stone huts. We dwell in clouds and sunshine way above the sea, our living in the sheep we milk and eat and the birds that we take from the cliffs. Though fishes abound, we do not go after them in boats because there is no protected cove or inlet with sloping sand for launching and hauling them to safety. Whenever the sea is at rest, we net fish among the rocks. That is also when a boat may draw close or depart without danger from the lashing waves, although it must still clear the surrounding ledges. That is the High Island."

"But is it the Last Island?" she kept asking.

I could not answer. Among my mother's people there was talk of an island in the sea where some do live through the ages, but I think it is beneath the water.

"Are you from the dead?" she then wanted to know.

Am I? What does it mean to come from the dead? Father says that when the sickness seized me I lay close to death for many days. Yet I lived. My mother, who was sick as well, did not live. My father's mother and father are dead now, too. Are not we all from those who once lived and live no longer?

The old woman is called Great Mother. She is said to know everything. But I do not think that is so, although she may be wise. She presses me to supply some clue to what she seeks to discover. Her questions ebb and flow. I try to please her, to satisfy her craving to understand. But I cannot.

She does not fear me, though, and she is not unkind. But her puzzlement seems to distract her, so that small matters slip from her thoughts before she can attend to them. She tends to lose the things she starts to bring to me. She forgets my name. She tells me to become acquainted with this place and these people in case I am welcomed.

But welcome is not at hand. Neither is banishment or death. So for now I dwell in solitude among these anxious folk, not unlike the dogs that live on the fringes of their settlement.

There are sand mounds where I walk. Despite the coarse long grasses rooted in them, they are soft and loose, so that my good leg sinks deep as I drag the twisted one along. The only sand I knew before lies beneath the water in a few rocky coves at one end of the High Island. We carried the sea sand up to be used to sharpen digging bones and cutting stones and to scour the floors of our houses.

I have not seen how this dry sand is used by these people. It is finer than the sea-packed sand at home. When I stoop to grab some, it warms my hands even as it runs between my fingers, as quick and free as water.

This day the wind-darkened sea tumbles about, leaping against outlying rocks that fling it back upon itself. The stack that rears up from the water holds birds in every crevice, different kinds on different levels. Except for that tall stack, the outlook is not so different from the one I am accustomed to. Only here there are fewer rocks offshore, and the seals do not come so close. Also, I cannot see as far because I am so low.

There is a cliff at the far end of the visible land. It seemed quite high when our boat came around it, although it is not so steep as the High Island cliffs. It is some distance from this beach and from the underground houses that cluster together on the inland slope above the sand mounds. It is too far for me to reach until my strength returns.

I mean to walk upon those sandy hills until I can stand no longer. Then I will rest awhile and watch the birds and seals and sheep. After that I will force myself to walk some more. This way my good leg will recall its purpose and gain anew the strength to do the work of two.

Then I shall set out for that cliff. Being there may make me feel as though I am home.

WILLOW

Willow came upon a strange-looking sodden heap. At first glance it resembled the limp carcass of a newborn lamb. Usually when she stumbled on one of those tiny dead creatures, nothing much remained but its shaggy skin. But this shapeless thing wasn't lying on the beach or half buried in the coarse dune grass. It had been tossed amid the general floor litter destined for the shell heap behind the huts.

She picked it up gingerly and shook it out. It still resembled an empty lambskin, although it retained the hint of the body it had covered. It was saturated with water and slippery to the touch, and it bore a peculiar sour smell that she didn't recognize.

It came to her that this was the garment the boy had worn and asked for. Holding it far from her own body, she carried it out into the sunshine, spread it to dry, and covered it with loose stones so that the wind wouldn't fling it away.

She went to the work place to tell Thorn that it was safe, but he wasn't there. Instead she found Great Mother in the doorway addressing Father and the uncles. Great Mother spoke of disconnections, of misgivings. She said that the boy's place among them would not be clear until they knew what came unseen with him. If he was one of the Boundless, like Star, he would not be with them for long.

"How will we know?" asked Uncle Redstone.

"The forthcoming birth could determine much about him.

If both Mizzle and her infant live, that will be a sign. If the infant is an unflawed girl, the sign will be great and clear, and you must serve the boy, since through him the People of the Singing Seals may thrive once again."

"And if the infant is like so many before it and never takes a breath?" he asked.

Great Mother shook her head. "Do not speak that thought. You invite death. Such words clear a space that death is quick to fill. I have already told you that we must wait and see, and then we may have to wait again until we understand what we are meant to do." She paused. "He may have come for me, this boy," she murmured. Her bony shoulders sagged with weariness as if the very process of understanding sapped her strength.

Her voice dropped to a whisper. "Always I have struggled to piece together the story of our people. You know that when the Wave swept away all who could sing the old songs, it ravaged our story, leaving only tattered shreds like the splintered remnants of boats and huts."

Great Mother's lament struck a sad and unsettling note. It filled Willow's throat with dread, for it expressed to the men how much was forever beyond her reach and theirs.

Usually Great Mother could unravel the most twisted of events and conditions. When she taught Willow the puzzling fragments of their people's story, she didn't shy away from unfinished endings. Instead she reminded Willow that even if they never retrieved the whole past, awareness of the unseen could enhance what they grasped, so long as they did not interpret in haste. Understanding took time and patience.

Recently Great Mother had remarked with a smile that each of them lacked what the other possessed. While she herself had little time left, Willow had little patience. So each must help the other.

Willow slipped away quietly before she was noticed. Outside she caught a glimpse of Tall Reed casting her eyes about to see who was at work and who was not. So Willow trudged up to her pile of roots and stems. Sinking down, she began to peel off the unneeded tendrils and branches. When she had cleaned off an armful, she carried it over the dunes and down to the water's edge. Here she shoved the fibers beneath the surface, holding them until her hands went numb.

Glancing around to make sure she was not watched, she straightened, clasping the soaked fibers against her. If Tall Reed saw her now, she would be made to keep the fibers under water much longer or else be told to take them inside and lay them in the stone vat where limpets were left to soften for bait. Tall Reed would remind her that softening could not be hastened.

Willow looked for a hollow in the dunes where she would be sheltered from Tall Reed's probing eyes as well as from the wind. Settling down in the sun-warmed sand, she spread out the roots. They were too stiff to be knotted together. But if no one noticed her at this work, she could alternate the more supple stems with the roots, using her teeth to pull each knot tight. As the bottom of the net began to take shape, she drew up her knees so they could help to flare the sides.

She realized that she should have carried two bundles of roots and stems. That way the next batch could soak in the shallows under a rock and she wouldn't have to risk attracting attention when she had to fetch another bundle. If she was seen, she might be sent to work on one of the large communal nets with the women.

No doubt Hazel was already at that work. She never seemed to make the women cross, not even when the knotting wore her fingers so raw that she had to be given a different task. In some way that Willow didn't understand, Hazel had already become one of the women.

Willow paused to rub her own fingers where the salt-water-soaked fibers raised welts on her callused skin. Then she continued with the knotting. If she pressed on, she would have one small net ready for finishing by dark.

That would be the time to let her crafting be seen. In the flickering light of the fire it might go unnoticed that she had interspersed stems with the roots. Approval of her quick work could gain her favor, and that might be reflected in the portion of meat she would be given.

But Willow's shortcut had not gone unnoticed. Setting aside the started net and rising to her feet, she found herself face to face with the boy, Thorn. It was unsettling. She had a feeling he had been watching her for some time. Watching her at the net-making.

His dark hair blew across his face without quite shielding his eyes. He had to brace himself against the wind as the loose sealskin garment he had been given flapped against his knees. Clutching his pouch as if for support, he said, "Those knots will not hold for long."

"Long enough," she retorted. "Long enough to catch the fish that hide in the sea grass. Anyway, most of the nets are soon torn."

He said, "I should think so, if they are woven like that."

Woven. She supposed it was a way of saying that something was poorly made. She considered ignoring his remark.

She considered pretending that she knew what "woven" meant. But the urge to understand compelled her to say, "That is not one of our words."

He frowned in puzzlement. Then he said, "What? Weaving?"

It wasn't exactly how she had heard him say it before, but she nodded.

They continued to face each other, silent now, mulling the vast gulf that had opened between them, although they were no more than three paces apart.

Muttering that she would be back, she turned from him and went to renew her supply of roots and stems. It wasn't until she walked past the garment spread out to dry that it occurred to her that she hadn't told him where it was. So she picked it up and stuffed it between two more bundles of fibers, then ran back to the dunes.

She found Thorn sitting above her hollow with his good leg outstretched, his shrunken leg angled awkwardly to the side. When she dropped the garment in front of him, he seized it as though he expected it to fly off like a captive bird.

She moved on to the water's edge and began the soaking process. When one bundle had been immersed just long enough, she trapped the other under a flat rock and returned to her started net.

Thorn had gone off somewhere. She didn't give him another thought, for the roots were not nearly softened, and it took all her strength and determination to force them to interlock with the stems. But she struggled on, yanking each knot fiercely even though she lost more than one connection and had to spit out bits of the root she had clenched between her teeth.

At last, defeated, she left what remained of her raw materials strewn about while she went to fetch the other bundle from the shallows. Perhaps these roots would knot more readily.

When she returned with them, she found Thorn kneeling in her hollow, crouched over the net-making materials. All she could think was that he would spoil her work. He glanced up at her and then down. She scrambled and slid to him, ready to snatch back her things. She saw that he wielded a shiny black stone with which he sliced a root lengthwise.

"What are you doing?" she demanded. "I need those. I have to soak them some more."

"Wait," he said with quiet concentration. "You will have them, and more." The sharp edge of the stone bore down on the stiff root, parting one section and then another from the whole.

The root was ruined, its cut end fanned out. She would never be able to knot a stem to it now. "You go away," she told him. "Somewhere else." But where could he go? He could barely walk.

At last he swiveled and shifted his body. "Like this," he said, pulling another long fiber from the main body of the root. "You can separate these while I start the next one."

"No," she objected. "No next one. I need to finish this."

He fixed her with a look she couldn't fathom. Those dark, dark eyes. How could he possibly belong to the People of the Singing Seals? Her people had long legs and light hair and blue eyes. No wonder he made her father and uncles uneasy. He made her uneasy, too.

Thorn proffered the split root, but she would not touch it. So he took it away with him, along with the garment. With his departure, he carried off her energy and resolve as well. She sat awhile, dreamy, distracted. Then, recalling her task, she resumed her work.

Everyone favored the greening time because of its almost endless days. But Willow also welcomed approaching night, when the sun poured seaward and brightness leached from the sky. Long before true darkness quenched the lingering light, the air cooled and the blue-gray water deepened with mystery. This was the time when the dogs went slinking off to hunt and the sheep wandered in from the rocks to bed down in the dunes. And it was when the people made their way to the thick-walled huts and stirred the smoldering embers to life.

But this evening the dogs hovered near the shell heaps, and the restless sheep stood about the beach.

Willow met Thistle and Crab lugging armfuls of dried sea wrack to feed the fires. They would all eat well, they told her, for the incoming tide had trapped two sheep, which had drowned. This night everyone would feast on the meat.

Already dogs were snarling over parts of the animals that had been thrown aside. From within the huts Uncle Redstone could be heard berating someone for undue waste. Instinctively the boys and Willow hung back from the passageway. Then Thistle turned and entered the work place. Willow and Crab followed.

"The boy is gone," said Thistle, staring into Thorn's corner.

"I saw him," Willow replied. "More than once."

They gazed at the empty corner as if it could reveal something about the boy.

Thistle said, "If he comes from the Last Island, it must be that part of him was left behind. The leg is still dead."

Crab said, "It might yet come. If we watch him, we might see it happen."

Willow remained silent. It was hard to reconcile the boy who had intruded into her hollow and shredded her root with one of the Boundless who could pass from death to life.

Someone called for the fuel the boys were supposed to bring to the fire, and they hurried out of the work place. Willow, deep in thought, left more slowly.

Smoke from the singed carcasses already filled the passage. Before the tantalizing smell of cooking meat assailed her, she reversed her direction and headed outdoors. In the sooty twilight, distances were deceptive and images distorted. Willow stared hard at what seemed to be a pack of dogs that had converged on a single object. Then she saw an arm thrust high above the moving mass of animals. Knowing that dogs crazed from hunger or fighting might turn on a person, she dashed forward, shouting at the dogs to back off.

Most of them did, cowering as they retreated from Thorn. Then they halted to eye him with the beginning of a renewed challenge. But one dog held its position, a foreleg still clasping what appeared to be a sheepskin. Or was it the boy's garment? No, the boy was wearing his garment. Willow drew closer. A cursory glance at the boy himself revealed no dog bites, no wounds of any kind. Nor did he seem alarmed or frightened.

"I took the skin to look it over," Thorn told her. "These dogs thought I took it for them. I was going to put it back. Maybe they would have dragged it down anyhow. They were trying to, which is how I came to see it." He broke off. Then, leaning down to the brown and black dog beside him, he pried its jaws open and firmly raised its foreleg. The dog, which had only one ear, and that one mutilated, submitted to this handling. Yielding to Thorn, it pulled itself onto its haunches and fixed him with an expectant look.

Willow glanced around, hoping someone else had witnessed this boy's surprising mastery of the dog. What would Great Mother make of it?

As Thorn struggled to rise, the other two dogs lurched toward him. He snatched up the skin and pulled from it a few scraps of fat, which he tossed over the dogs' heads. Even as they dove for those bits, he dropped another morsel in front of the dog crouched before him. Staggering to gain his precarious footing, he extended the sheepskin toward Willow.

Without thinking, she received it, then quickly scanned the area to locate the other one. There it was, draped across the top of a stone pile. It always surprised her how much heavier the skin of a freshly killed animal was than one fully dried. She slung it as high as she could before turning back to the boy to tell him that if he wasn't careful he could become the dogs' next meal.

But she had to deliver this warning while the black and brown dog, its ragged ear lying flat against its head, was licking Thorn's fingers clean.

"There," he said quietly to the dog, withdrawing his hand. It was the only word he spoke to it. Yet the dog rose and followed him to the stone pile as though commanded. Thorn hobbled slowly, his awkward gait twisting his entire body with every step.

When he was close enough to touch the skin, his fingers probed and crept. Then he turned to Willow in puzzlement.

"It is sheep?"

"Yes, sheep," she confirmed. What else could it be?

"What happened to the wool?" he asked.

"I do not know," she said. Then she added, "I do not know what you mean."

He said, "You pluck wool from sheep and then you spin it and weave it. This," he told her, pointing to his tunic, "this is made from sheep wool."

"Oh." All at once Willow understood. "The hair. Sometimes we use the sheep hair when we make ropes, but mostly we use the whole skin for warmth, like the sealskin they gave you to wear."

Thorn sank down beneath the draped skins. "Everything is different here," he said, suddenly looking weary, dejected.

"There will be a feast soon," Willow told him. She was about to urge him to come inside with her when she recalled Great Mother's pronouncement about contact with others, especially Mizzle. "Go to your corner in the work place, and in a while someone will bring you meat."

"In a while," he repeated, making no effort to pull himself up again.

She left him then. Already the air was heavy with the promise of the feast. It had been a long day, much of it bewildering. She was ready for the closeness of the hut, her own people, a full stomach, sleep.

ᐱ THORN

I have my tunic again. It smells of home. The sealskin garment is not much more than a sack slit down the sides with a head opening at the top, but it will serve as well as our sheepskins for an outside covering when the wind blows cold. The sheep here grow hair instead of wool and seem to live off the weed that washes in on the tide.

I have been watching them pick their way along the off-shore rocks, often at the mercy of waves or rising water. When they drown, they are eaten. The meat is dark and does not taste like ours. Nothing is familiar to me.

Father could not have known what these people would be like, for he never saw them until he brought me here. He preferred that I be given to them than to the sea, but the only knowledge he possessed was from his father's tales. He expected I would be welcome. He believed I would thrive.

Yet I think they may not keep me. They speak of the Last Island, of the Boundless, and I cannot tell what they want of me. I may be given to the sea after all.

I watched the girl, Willow, knotting roots and stems for a net. I tried to show her how to make it stronger, but she thought I would spoil it. I need a shoulder sling so I can move about with both hands free. After I pull some roots and braid the strands into a length of rope for a sling to carry my pouch, maybe she will notice and decide to learn.

It is strange to be alone at night, to hear no sounds of

others. Last night while I slept my mother visited me, as she sometimes did in times gone by. I heard her voice, and then I felt her arms. I tried to tell her that I am no longer the little child she once held, but my voice would not come. When I reached out to her, I woke to find a dog pressed against me. I could tell it was the one-eared dog who was sharing his warmth. He slept beside me until dawn, and then he went away before the people in the huts began to stir.

The dogs eat whatever is thrown outside and keep the settlement clean, but they are kept from the dwellings. Nor are they used to gather the sheep as our dogs do. They are more wild than ours, except for the one that seems to favor me.

He follows me now, although he keeps a wary distance. Still, I have only to look up to find him tracking me across the sand.

WILLOW

Toward midday the wind shifted. It brought moisture on the air and blurred the horizon.

The uncles and Willow's father decided to take advantage of this change before true fog clamped down on the shore and held them captive. They collected their strongest ropes, discarding those that had been frayed on rocks during the last hunt. The repaired ones that were spliced might be used as well, but everyone knew they increased the risk of loss when the boys were lowered from the steep, overhanging cliff.

Willow couldn't stay away from these preparations. Since everyone knew she could climb as well as Thistle and Crab, she harbored the secret hope that she might yet be directed toward one of the tree-boats.

But Great Mother's arrival on the beach ended Willow's chances. "No need to stand about," she told Willow. "There's women's work to be done."

Tall Reed had already gathered the few children strong enough to carry water. She eyed Willow, thought a moment, and told her to continue with her net-making. Ready for a change, any change, Willow said she and Hazel together could manage the big containers. But Tall Reed looked askance at any offer coming from Willow. "You work better by yourself," she said. And then she added, "Hazel and the others work better without you."

So Willow went off on her own.

Great Mother was walking up from the shore as Willow, a bundle under each arm, headed for the dunes.

"You can knot the nets right here," Great Mother said.

Unable to think of an acceptable argument, Willow halted, but without turning back to the huts.

Great Mother looked at her, then shook her head. "If only you did not resist what you are, then trouble would not be your constant companion. It is because no mother reared you," she said. "It is because your father took you everywhere, as though you were a boy."

Willow said, "Tall Reed liked my knot work. I did more than the others."

"You are quick," Great Mother told her. "Quick to learn, quick to finish. But that is not the whole of work."

"Then why not let me do what is most needed? Nesting time will soon be past, and neither boy is as skilled and light as I am. I can gather more birds."

"It is time for you to grow big and heavy. That is how women carry babies through lean times. If our people cannot make new lives, we cannot survive. Unless you prepare for what you must be, all you have learned from me will wither before it can flower." Great Mother paused. "Surely you have noticed that as I grow forgetful, I lose the people's confidence. So the next Keeper of Story may be needed before I am gone from here. You know that."

"But when you go, maybe you will return," said Willow. "Like the boy, like Thorn."

Great Mother shook her head. "You do not know that he is Boundless and from the Last Island. That is what the men want to believe, for it gives them hope to think he is like Star. They do not consider that it may be false hope."

The old woman's sharpness caught Willow by surprise, though she knew it shouldn't have. Great Mother didn't think like others. She mulled and probed and questioned every mystery. Had Willow herself been swept along by those who were beginning to view Great Mother's forgetfulness as wisdom turned sour?

"How will we know?" Willow asked. "When will we know?"

Great Mother shrugged. "We must keep listening and looking. And even if we do, we may not be certain. If the boy comes from the Last Island, then where are all the people taken by the Wave and devoured by the sea? Where are the father and mother of his father? It may be that the boy is only a maimed child clinging to survival."

"The dogs—" Willow broke off. She had been about to say that the dogs feared him, but that wasn't exactly true. So she turned the thought around and said, "He does not fear the dogs."

"Do you mean that he is careless of them as you were when you walked inland alone on the hillside?"

Willow said, "Not careless. I think there is trust between him and the dogs."

Great Mother said, "Do not think too highly of it, lest the trust be misplaced. After all, the boy may be a fool."

Willow considered her dealings with Thorn. She didn't mention his meddling or the shiny stone that cut so fine a fiber. "Must I still be wary of him?" she asked. "May I touch what he touches?"

"Be somewhat wary. But spend a little time with him and hear what he has to say of the High Island. Although I have spoken with him, I think he may be more free with you than he is with an old woman."

"Should Crab and Thistle talk with him as well?" Willow asked.

Great Mother frowned. "Maybe," she said. "They are curious about him. But I think they are too much like little children who prod the netted fish to make it squirm. Go along now," she ordered, sounding suddenly tired of Willow.

Willow wondered whether this meant that after all she was allowed to take her work to the dunes. She didn't ask, though. She simply acted on the dismissal and went.

The next time Willow caught sight of Thorn, he was making his tortured way back from the direction of the headland, a distant bobbing figure that caught her eye because of the object that bounced along beside him. As he drew near, she could see that it was his pouch, which dangled from some kind of sturdy string that crossed from his shoulder to his side and swung with his lurching gait.

Going to meet him, Willow assumed that Thorn had picked up one of the damaged ropes that had been discarded. But when she was closer, she saw that his sling was unlike any rope she had ever seen.

Thorn said, "They have all gone to the tall rock for birds?"

"The stack, yes," she said. "They choose a time when there is some light but little sun. Shadows warn the birds." Then she asked, "What kind of rope is that? Did you bring it from the High Island?"

"I made it here," he told her. "It is from the same kind of roots you use." He nodded toward the started net in her hands.

She touched the sling. Since he didn't draw back or object,

she set down her net and with both hands took hold of the twisted rope he wore.

"Wait," he said, lifting it over his head and then handing it to her. "Try to break it. You will find it strong."

She glanced at him doubtfully, then yanked hard. When nothing happened, she bent it double. It remained whole, unmarred. She raised it to her nose. It smelled like her net, like her hands, like all the roots she had been knotting. Yet it was transformed, somehow tougher while at the same time supple. What crafting power could make such a thing? Could it be dangerous? What would Great Mother think?

"How?" Willow asked, returning the sling to him.

"I started to show you," he told her.

"No, you were spoiling ..." Her voice fell away. Had some marvel passed before her eyes without her seeing it? "Show me again," she demanded.

They headed for her hollow, Willow outdistancing him and pausing repeatedly to let him catch up. For the first time she noticed how his face clenched as he dragged the thin, crooked leg, leaning first one way and then the other to maintain his forward movement. It crossed her mind that a person so skewed could not possibly have anything to offer to one who was complete and strong. What might he demand from her in exchange for his skill? Would he take her strength? A limb?

Think of waking up in the morning to find herself maimed and broken! Had it happened that way to Thorn?

He couldn't keep up with her. Before reaching the hollow in the dunes, he sank to his good knee and then all the way down. His sweat-soaked hair clung to his face and neck. She stood uncertainly a few paces ahead and saw how his hands trembled as they pulled his leg around from behind.

"I will come," he said. "Soon."

The one-eared dog appeared out of nowhere and stretched out beside him. There was something unnerving about that closeness, another sign that Thorn was unlike all the people Willow had known before.

Without approaching, she spoke to him. "Did you ever walk like ... others?"

"I did. Walked, ran, jumped. Everything."

"Did you wake up one morning and discover that leg?" Pointing to it, she shivered.

"I sickened," he said. "There is not much I can tell you about it, except that I saw others sicken before me. My mother ... I saw my mother sleep and sleep. She would not awaken. Then I ... Then the sickness squeezed my head and neck and back until I could not move, could not swallow, could not catch my breath. There is little to say, for I was far away then, far, far away. Long afterward I came back. Changed."

"Came back from the Last Island? You were Boundless." It was a kind of confirmation.

"Was I?" He sounded baffled. "It felt like waking."

Willow shivered again. "You woke to find that you had returned without your proper leg."

"When I woke," he told her, "I knew nothing about the leg. There were many small wakings before, finally, waking into change."

"To the wrong leg," said Willow.

"No," he replied, "to find my mother gone. At first all I could do was shut my eyes tight against the glare of daylight. So I listened for her voice. I could not hear it. At each waking I listened. Finally I looked. She was not there. She was not anywhere."

Willow scowled in bewilderment. How could his mother be gone if they had both traveled to the Last Island? "She was not where you were?" Willow asked.

"She was not," Thorn said bleakly.

"And the leg?" Willow prompted.

He shrugged. "It was there. For a while I did not know there was anything amiss with me. I was shifting my leg with my hands long before I thought about it, before I understood."

Willow, who had never known her mother, couldn't fathom how a person who was able to recall so clearly the loss of a mother had barely registered the loss of a leg.

The fog bank hovered out at sea, a presence no one could ignore. Everyone knew how swiftly it could swell and roll landward, so the uncles and Willow's father cast their eyes toward it as they plied the tree-boats between the stack and the shore.

Before Willow could make it back to her hollow and Thorn, she was called, along with Hazel, and told to carry birds to the drying racks on the windward side of the settlement. After that the girls were sent to fetch dried weed for the outdoor fire and fresh water from the stream.

When they filled a slender stone pot and placed it over the flames, it sizzled and popped and then cracked, springing leaks around its base that doused the fire. The women fussed. Some ordered the girls to fetch a thicker pot that could take the heat; others told them to get out of the way.

Willow chose to heed this second command. She raced back to her hollow, where she found Thorn engrossed in something of his own making. He used a small polished bone with a sharply slanted tip and a hole in the opposite end through which a string was threaded. The bone drew the string over and under nearly rigid riblike stems. After every completed round, he paused to press the encircling string against the previous strand.

"Is it a basket?" she asked.

"A basket and net in one," he told her. "When it is finished, I will show you how to use it."

As she watched he changed the order of his binding. At the following round there was a small space followed by two more dense rounds and then another space.

"I want to try," she said.

He looked up appraisingly. He squirmed backward to make room for her as she slid into the hollow. "Next," he told her, "the ribs must be lengthened. Like this." He pulled the black stone from his pouch and began to shave off fibers from a root.

Seized with impatience, she objected. She wanted to use the bone thing.

He didn't respond, just kept shredding the root until it was separated into individual fibers.

She supposed she might as well be lugging water and gaining approval from the women, but she stayed on. Surely it would not be long before she would be wielding the bone with the string.

When Thorn was finished, he rubbed the stone on his tunic before replacing it in his pouch. "What kind of stone is it?" she asked, thinking it looked like black ice.

"It is fire stone. It comes from fire in the earth."

"Do you mean if I dig a pit and bring fire to it, I can make a stone with such a shine and edge?"

"No one makes it," he told her. "The mountain heaves it up when it burns."

Incredulous, she asked, "What is the mountain? Have you seen this fire?"

He shook his head. "But the men who saved my father's father and mother came from a land with a mountain that burned. Also, they called the High Island a mountain on the sea." Noting her scowl of confusion, he paused. "Look," he told her, pointing to the headland with its coastal cliff. "That is high where it faces the sea. The whole of the High Island is like that, only taller. Not like this." He swept his arm in a wide arc, describing the gentle descent of the land through the dunes to the sea.

"There are high places here, too," she said. "They are called hills."

"The High Island has hills as well. But I think a mountain is more like the stack where the birds nest, only greater in extent. Fire boils up from deep inside. That is what those men told my father's father. They had stones like the one they gave to him, which he gave to my father, who gave it to me. Now," Thorn said, "it is mine, and I have used it to prepare the pieces we will braid together."

He swiveled around so that he was beside her. Then he laid out three fibers stripped from the root, knotted them together at one end, and drew his knee up so that he could hook the end on his big toe. Then he pulled the fibers taut and begin to fold them over one another.

She said, "It is something like binding our hair to keep it out of our faces."

"It is," he agreed. "But the purpose is different. The pieces are as fine as they can be. It takes a long time, especially if the finished lengths are then applied in the same way. Thick or thin, the resulting strand is always stronger than it looks."

After a while he handed the strands to Willow. She did what she had seen him do until she paused to brush a lock of her hair from her eyes. Then she lost track of which strand came next. He reached past her and unraveled them.

"Don't," she exclaimed. "We will never finish."

"You will only finish if you do it properly," he said. "Otherwise it will loosen. It will not hold its shape."

With a sigh she set to work again, this time gaining in confidence and speed.

Again he stopped her. Again he showed her where two strands were crossed together. Again he pulled her work apart.

She could barely contain herself. He was as demanding as Great Mother. When would she come to the part with the bone? But she continued until Thorn took the nearly finished braid from her.

Slowly, methodically, he attached the loose ends to the feathered tip of one rib, extending it and bending it so it flared out. When he explained that this had to be done to each rib, Willow could bear it no longer.

"Later," she told him. "After I haul more water. And they may want me for other work."

Yes, later, she thought as she raced across the dunes and back to the outdoor fire. She would return to Thorn when he was ready for her to use the bone. Meanwhile she might as well share in the women's efforts to prepare the birds. If she resumed her work alongside Hazel, maybe her brief absence would be forgotten, or at least forgiven.

When the two uncles who brought birds to shore stayed to make more rope, their women went to help soften the stiff, unyielding sealskins. Willow joined them. But before the women and Willow had managed to flatten and stretch just one skin and examine it for flaws, the uncles started to cut along the outer edges of others. Kneeling and bearing down hard with their sharpest stones, the uncles cut in a spiral fashion from the outside edge toward the center, until they could peel away continuous strips of skin.

The women objected. What gain was there in those long strips if the finished rope held treacherous thin spots?

The uncles insisted that these skins were sound. Ropes were needed out on the bird cliffs, needed at once, before the fog put an end to the hunt.

The women kept chivvying them. What was the matter with the ropes they had already taken? Had the ropes given way? If they had already failed, maybe it was because they too had been made in haste. Were the boys injured? Were they well?

Willow held her breath. If just one of the boys could no longer scale the cliffs, she would present herself as a spare climber.

"They are well," said one uncle. "You fret for nothing."

The other said, "Go back to the drying racks. We can deal with the skins."

Their women backed off but didn't leave. Willow saw how their presence galled the men. Where the skin resisted first cuts, the uncles applied their stones with fiercer thrusts, with greater abandon. Willow knew how those cutting stones were used. All her life she had watched them being shaped by other stone tools. All her life she had seen them kill and slice and flay. Looking at them now, though, she thought of Thorn's fire stone. She could almost feel the hard, gleaming surface, smooth as black ice. Could its sharp edge, capable of parting one thin fiber from another, also slice through tough skin?

"See there," one of the women declared. "There." She pointed to a careless slash across a strip. "That is how a rope breaks. That is how we lose our sons."

Grumbling, the men swiveled on their knees to block the women's scrutiny.

After the women left, Willow waited a little longer. Without being prompted, she raised one finished end of sealskin rope and worked it over a stone slab. Bit by bit the rope stretched and softened. When she came to a thick lump, she sawed it back and forth over the slab, then tried chewing it to flatten it out. The uncles noted her efforts without comment. By the time they were ready to gather up the sealskin coils, she had still not resolved the lump.

"It will do no harm," one uncle told her. He yanked the strip on either side of the lump to show how strong it was.

Willow said, "I would gladly go down the cliff bound to this rope. Any rope."

The uncle said, "I would gladly bring you if Great Mother did not object."

Willow couldn't resist pressing him. "You know I am light on a rope. You know how quick I am."

He hesitated. Then he shook his head. "Only if Great Mother allows it," he told her. He turned and followed the other uncle down to the shore.

Willow gazed after them. Then, instead of returning to the women preparing the birds, she picked up a few scraps

59

of discarded sealskin and sauntered after the men. She was more than halfway there when she caught sight of Thorn half sitting, half rolling, as he dragged a tree-boat onto the beach. One uncle gave a shout and broke into a run. By the time Willow reached them, Thorn had already been thrust aside and the uncles were shoving off into the water.

The lower half of Thorn's tunic was dripping. He said, "They fear my touch. They must think my hand taints their boats."

"What were you doing with the tree-boat?" she asked.

"It was floating off," he told her. "When I stood up to move about, to make myself stronger, I saw it bobbing at the water's edge. By the time I got there I had to wade out to catch it."

Willow was on the verge of disputing this. The uncles took no chances with their boats. But she choked back her retort. Maybe this time the uncles had been careless because of being pressed to deliver the birds and return to the stack with fresh rope.

Or did Thorn cause the mishap? Was it a sign of trouble ahead?

He seemed unconcerned as he gazed seaward. Willow saw that he was tracking the movements of a seal, which seemed to have fixed him in its sight as well. This was very strange. Usually when the tree-boats were out on the water, the seals were nowhere to be seen.

The seal started its mournful croon. Thorn stood ankle-deep in foam and rockweed, leaning to one side for balance, intent only on the seal.

Willow barely heard his answering call. He was so still and the sound was so hushed that her first thought was that another seal nearby must be calling to the one facing him. But the seal knew. It seemed to stand straight up from the water, its nostrils distended, its huge, wet eyes fastened on Thorn.

Splashing into the shallows, Willow turned to watch and listen, only to find everything changed. The seal had vanished, leaving in its place a small tuck on the calm surface of the sea.

Thorn stood a moment longer in utter silence. Then, stumbling, he lurched back to land.

THORN

After three long days I completed the net. Often Willow tired of the work. She could not see a reason for the many tasks that slowed the making. I have known young children who turn away like that, running off and returning, as if borne to and fro on changing winds.

When at last we went together to try the finished net, she was amazed at how it kept its shape. The nets these people make must be constantly pried open lest they collapse and then tangle. So the people are fortunate in their fishing ground. With few rocks to avoid, netting fish in open shallows is nothing like the task at home.

After I weighted the sturdy bottom of our net with small stones, I showed Willow how to capture tiny fish and then hold them there by pulling the net steadily along. Soon a well-grown fish had darted in after them. By the time I had snatched it out and flung it onto the sand, another fish was nosing its way into the net.

When she had grown used to plying the net in this fashion, I left her to it. After I have been with her like this, I feel as though I had walked beyond endurance and must drag myself to a quiet hollow to recover my strength.

Now that I am able to send food to the fire, maybe the people will look on me with favor. Meanwhile they have walled off the corner of the work place so that when I sleep I am truly alone. Only the dog slinks through the narrow opening to be with me. Sometimes I am already asleep and wake to feel him beside me. Sometimes he follows in my footsteps, and we bed down together.

The night the fog came in we both awoke to the howling. The dog added his voice to those outside the huts. As I drew myself up to listen I heard the distant song of many seals. Dogs answered, sometimes urgently, sometimes gently. From time to time my companion whimpered or moaned. After a while I sank back down to sleep.

At home the seals that visit the High Island rocks do not sing. Still, they come and speak with me through their eyes. Here the seals give voice and seem to want my echoing croon. Are they different in other ways? I see no young here, even though it is pupping time for our seals. I have begun to look for the singing seals whenever I gaze seaward. They tend to keep their distance, hauling out beyond the stack on ledges that only emerge when the tide is low. Sometimes, though, one or more will approach and even follow as I try to walk along the shore.

I still cannot tell what the people here expect of me. Like most of the seals, they watch but keep their distance. The call I hear in the singing of the sea beasts reaches me more clearly than the words and ways of these people.

Only Willow talks with me. When she agreed to bring the net full of fine, well-grown fishes to her people, I helped her carry the load until we neared the huts. Then I dropped back, and she hauled the catch the rest of the way on her own. But I watched. The people circled the upstanding net as dogs do when they come upon an unfamiliar creature with a strange smell. Then they drew back and plied Willow with questions.

Staying out of their way, I was not able to hear what passed between them, but I believe their wariness was akin to dread. Still, I waited, prepared to come forward, to explain the crafting of the net to all of them. But I was not called. Maybe Willow tried to tell them why the net was made as it was. Maybe she said I could show them how to fashion others like it. Maybe. She did not look at me.

I was foolish to think they would be glad of the net we crafted. Willow had wanted to keep it from them, although each time she carried the fishes to her people, she gained in their regard. She gained, not I.

It seems more and more likely they will give me to the sea after all. Thoughts of my sister should hold me from fear. But when that first boat tipped me into the sea, I thrashed and gulped like a sheep that topples from the cliff and struggles in vain. If only I could forget how the sea that swallows you fills you with itself until you grow huge and shapeless, without voice or sight.

And here there is no one to lift me and carry me to land.

I look for Willow. Her chatter might drive off these thoughts. But the old woman has led her inland, and so I turn back to the dunes alone.

I continue to walk until my good leg trembles and gives way. Since I must remain where I fall, I seek the sand, for I can claw at it to carve out a small shelter, a leaning place.

The dog comes. He is a tireless digger. The sand flies up behind him. Soon we are nestled together, out of the wind.

WILLOW

Great Mother led Willow onto the heath. The fog had washed over the dormant flowers and swept a mass of tiny blooms into life. Willow was dazzled. Fragrance and color, clamorous bees, and small, frantic land birds abounded. Her steps faltered.

Great Mother wouldn't let her stop. "Mizzle will have her baby soon," she told Willow. She kept on walking as she spoke. "After that, if all goes well for her and the infant, the boy may be accepted. Until then, we are at risk, and so is he. A new life can bring hope to our dwindling people, so Mizzle must be shielded from him."

"Thorn knows to stay away from her," Willow replied. "He stays away from almost everyone."

"But this day he came with you. He came too close. The men find him meddling with their boat. They see the dog in thrall to him. They are desperate and would have him gone. All that prevents them from giving him to the sea is the possibility that he is from the Last Island and that if we do him no harm, then others of our lost ones may yet return." She sighed. "I wish I could say what they long to hear. I wish I believed that his father's mother and father were taken from a rock off our shore. But Willow, all the rocks were under water. No one could have clung to a rock. The Wave seized the land and hurled it back so that we no longer knew it."

Willow said, "And Thorn cannot say if he is Boundless,

although he believes the story about his father's mother and father. He knows little. But he is clever. He is a maker."

Great Mother nodded. "Yes, and just as his infirmity seems a taunt, a cruel reminder of all the flawed infants born to us, his cleverness unsettles our men. It is not fitting for him to show them new ways, better ways." She turned to face Willow. "You must see that."

"I suppose," Willow mumbled. She didn't, though. And if she did, what did Great Mother think she should do about it?

"If he could walk the distance," Great Mother said, "I would send him far from us. Even to the buried stones."

That brought Willow up short. The thought of sending Thorn there seemed monstrous. She watched Great Mother brush wisps of hair from her haggard face. Willow saw how sunken her old eyes were, how bleached, as if the spark within had dimmed even more since Willow had looked into them last.

"Why?" Willow asked her. "It could be a place of danger."

"But if the boy is Boundless, he may possess knowledge without realizing it. Being there might awaken it in him." Great Mother's voice dropped to a whisper. "There is no one else. There is no one but you to carry my scant knowledge forward. I hoped to live until you became a woman," she continued. "But this will not happen. Even if the boy holds our lost knowledge, and even if it were revealed through him, who but I could recognize it? And I might not. I might err. I might have erred all along."

A kind of panic seized Willow. Never before had Great Mother sounded defeated. If she began to doubt the truths that held all the People of the Singing Seals together, what remained? She could not err. She must not. "Maybe the baby will be a girl," Willow blurted. "And maybe after that another one will come. Maybe there will soon be many girls."

"Willow, I was very young when the Wave took our leaders, our Keeper of Story. Not many survived along with us children, a few women and fewer old men. I learned what I could from them, from recollections riddled with grief, from knowledge driven by desperation and fear. Did I learn wrong along with right?"

"No!" Willow insisted. "It is only weariness speaking through you."

Great Mother merely eyed her, disappointment in her gaze.

Willow knew she had failed her. This was far worse than disobedience. To protect herself from upheaval, she had rejected Great Mother's doubt, her plea to be heard. Ashamed now, Willow did not know how to repair what she had done. But she had to say something, to fill the silence between them. "If you thought of sending Thorn to the stones in the ground, that means you do believe that he comes from the Last Island."

Great Mother summoned her strength, her voice. "I have not told you everything," she said. "I have not told you that I have discovered shadow shapes from the time before the Wave. Just before the Wave overcame us, one of our people made a wave shape. I never saw it, but one woman did, and she said that once a shadow shape is released from the thing itself, it goes where it will, does what it will. Then we are powerless to contain it. Lately, though, I have wondered if she led us astray. I am no longer certain that shadow waves or shadow beasts bring forth such horrors. And once I cast doubt on one belief, other doubts come crowding after."

Determined not to fail her again, Willow met the pale, commanding eyes. After a moment words came to Willow as though recalled. "Then send the doubts away. They are shadows themselves, shadows cast by the one error. You do not have to admit them all into your thoughts."

Great Mother's expression softened for an instant. Then she continued, her voice rising and falling as she laid out her plan. "We have little time," she said. "Soon the boy should be removed from sight, from everyone's sight, until Mizzle gives birth."

Turning, she pointed in the direction of the hill down which Willow had rolled. "Beyond. The other side, but not all the way to the flat stones in the slope above the marsh. That is where the boy can stay until Mizzle has her baby. We will need skins and bones for a shelter. We should get them here within the next few days."

"My father and Uncle Redstone can carry many skins," Willow said.

Great Mother shook her head. "I would ask the men to help with this if they could do that much and no more. But fear of what they do not understand makes them rash. The less the boy is in their way, the safer he will keep."

Safe? thought Willow. Alone? She said, "You told me I was not safe from dogs. Thorn cannot even run."

"And I have seen the dogs follow him with their eyes. They sense his weakness. Still, with the one-eared dog at hand, they do not stalk him."

So Great Mother would rely on an old dog to protect Thorn against the pack? Willow wanted to object, but she was wary now. Afraid to say anything that would lead to discord, she gazed across the hill where wind-driven clouds in constant motion cast great, dark shapes that seemed full of life, like seals swimming and rolling, barely visible beneath the sun-struck water.

Great Mother was speaking again, pressing on about arrangements. So many skins. Used ones would do. Strong ribs and shoulder bones. Food. A digging stick? A few of the most vigorous women, along with the two older girls, if the boys were not back in time, ought to provide what was needed. Then it would be up to Willow to instruct Thorn. She would send or lead him to the stony slope facing the inland hills and looking away from the sea and the cluster of huts where Mizzle's baby would be born.

Willow nodded to show that she was ready to act swiftly, to accomplish what Great Mother demanded. She forced herself to lift her gaze from the tumbling cloud shadows that darkened the heath. Even so, she couldn't help noticing how those shifting shapes blotted out the color, driving the bright new blossoms to ground.

No sooner did Willow retrieve Thorn's net, which had been cast onto the refuse heap, than Crab confronted her. "Who will use it?" he asked.

She had intended to keep it, but all she said was, "It can lure and hold more and greater fish than the uncles catch in their nets."

Crab looked doubtful. For days now he and Thistle had been goading her with tales of their exploits bird-hunting on the stack. When Thistle's shredded rope had left him stranded on a shallow rock shelf, the men were unable to drop the end of a new rope down to him. So Crab, trailing a freshly cut rope, had been lowered to the overhang above him.

The boys' most recent account of this event had driven Willow into bitter silence.

"I could not see Thistle," Crab had informed his rapt audience, mostly small boys.

"I could not see Crab, but I knew he was above me," Thistle had told them. Then he had launched into the details of his ordeal, describing what it felt like to stand with his back flattened against the cliff and his head bent forward.

"I tried to dangle the rope straight down," said Crab, "but the wind blew it off."

"I had to reach out over the chasm without falling," Thistle said.

Hazel had clapped her hands to her ears. "Come," she had urged Willow. "We have heard this already. Be glad we were not there."

But Willow wasn't glad. Unlike the younger children, who were simply enthralled, she felt her torment increase with each breathtaking moment the boys described. Still, she couldn't bear to walk away while they embellished their story all over again.

Now, at last, she was almost in command. She possessed this marvelous object. She had only to convince Crab that a rare new power had crafted it. Then he would surely pass this on to Thistle. If only she could think of a way to hint that danger lurked in this power. He would see for himself that she was not afraid.

"Who caught all the fish you brought in it?" Crab asked.

Willow hesitated. If she claimed that achievement entirely for herself, it would weaken the impact of what she hoped to convey about Thorn.

"Who?" Crab demanded.

"The boy," she told him. "Thorn."

"Caught those fish all in one scoop? How could he? How do you know he did?"

"I was there," she said. "I saw him." Her thoughts raced to catch up to her words. "He can make things. I ..." She checked herself. It was prudent to give up her part in that making. "I saw him make some of it." She searched for the right, compelling words. "He called a spell upon it, named weaving."

"Weaving," Crab repeated. "A weaving spell. Do our uncles and fathers know of it? If so, why did they leave the net to rot?"

"They fear what they do not understand." These words, Great Mother's words, presented themselves to Willow.

Crab drew closer to see the strange net she held. "Give it to him. Let him show us."

Willow felt her mouth go dry. "If only there were time," she managed to reply. "But he is to be sent away from the sea. Great Mother said so. At once. You and Thistle are to bring things inland. The strongest children are to help."

She stood there holding Thorn's net, her thoughts scrambling to account for her having it. "Thorn's belongings must go with him," she told Crab. "And I have already carried this when it was heavy with fish." She was saying too much, but she didn't want to leave an opening for more questions. "Find Thistle. Tall Reed is gathering bones and skins. Go to her."

At last Crab nodded and turned away to do as she bid. Satisfied that she had succeeded in goading him into a mixture of curiosity and envy, she stood watching him disappear into the cluster of huts. Then she headed for the dunes to tell Thorn to ready himself for the inland trek.

She was elated. There would be no more talk of the perilous bird hunt on the stack. Thorn was the lure now. She wanted to run, to slide feet first into the steepest hollow. She wanted to leap from rock to rock above the shallows and then fling herself into the biggest foaming wave that broke at her. She feared nothing. Nothing!

She searched awhile, and then she resorted to calling. "Thorn, Thorn." But he didn't answer, didn't appear. Eventually she made her way back to the huts and into the work place, which was empty. She squeezed around the edge of the new wall into Thorn's corner. It, too, was empty, except for a few old skins in a heap.

As she turned to leave, she noticed, low down, scratches or fresh lines on the inside face of the stone. Squatting brought her closer, nearly eye-level with the markings, which even in the dimness assumed the shapes of things she knew. She could make out dogs, seals, and a face.

She felt her skin tighten the way it did if she plunged into icy water. Everything in her tensed, forcing her to back away. At the same time the figures held her entranced. She told herself she had to look again lest her eyes had tricked her into seeing what couldn't be.

The shapes remained, more recognizable than at first glance. Not even the clouds above the hill produced such likenesses. And these weren't fleeting. She could touch them if she dared, trace their outline with her finger.

She stared and stared. She shut her eyes, then opened them again. Each figure was just as it had been. She felt the jagged line that made a dog's chewed ear. It was as if the shadow of the black and brown dog that followed Thorn everywhere was here now on the stone. She rubbed the ear and for an instant it darkened, nearly vanished. Then it reappeared. Was this how it came to life?

On sudden impulse she dragged over the pile of skins and shoved them, along with the net, against the markings. Now, if anyone glanced in here, the dogs and the seal and the face would be less noticeable. Still, she herself had touched a forbidden thing. Was it akin to touching Thorn? Why had he scratched those figures and then left them in full view like that? What did they mean to him? What might they mean to Great Mother, who was beginning to doubt the people's horror of all shadow shapes?

Full of wonder, Willow squeezed through to the empty work place and out into full sunlight. Squinting against the glare, she nearly ran back inside for one more look at those shapes on the stone. Then she caught sight of Tall Reed bearing down on her.

They were ready to start, Tall Reed informed her. It was up to Willow to find Thorn and bring him along.

Willow caught sight of the dog first and guessed that Thorn must be nearby. Since it was pointless to call against the wind, she just kept trudging toward him through the long grass. Then, quite suddenly, Thorn sat up. He was facing seaward, only a few paces ahead. He hadn't heard her, but the dog had alerted him and he was just beginning to look around. He greeted her with a smile.

"I've been looking for you everywhere," she told him. "Why did you come all this way?"

"The headland is high. It is more like home," he said. "I have not yet been to the summit, but each day I get a bit farther."

"Well," she blurted, "you must go farther now, only in another direction."

He looked puzzled. "What direction is that?"

She pointed inland.

He said, "I have never been away from the sight and sound of the sea."

"It is only until Mizzle's baby is born," she told him, wondering as she spoke whether this was entirely true.

"Are we all going?" he asked.

Willow looked away. "Some of us," she replied. "For now." She considered explaining Great Mother's plan, but there was time enough for that as they went along. Besides, his eyes held a troubled look. At best it would be a struggle for him to walk that distance without reluctance slowing him as well.

But he had expended all his energy getting partway to the headland and was in no condition to start on this new trek at once. When she realized how spent he was, she asked him whether there was anything that could help.

"Something to lean on," he told her. "Like the oar I used the first day."

"It is made of tree, like the boats. The trees are a long way off."

"Bone, then," he said. "A straight bone to match my leg."

"Rest here," she told him. "I will come back with something."

She started off at a run, but she couldn't keep it up. What a pair they would make, worn out before they started.

Back at the settlement she rummaged through the outer layer of shells and then went to look inside, starting with her father's hut. Uncle Redstone came in behind her and asked her what she sought. She explained. He didn't think she would find a bone to bear a boy's weight.

"He is not very big," she reminded the uncle. Then she introduced a note of urgency. "Great Mother wants him away from here at once, but he cannot go far without an oar or something like it to help him along."

Uncle Redstone thought a moment. He glanced at bone implements; he fingered a curved sheep rib. Then he reached up to the roof, testing bone beams until he came to one that could be removed and replaced. He slid a straight, smoke-blackened bone back and forth until it was loose enough to be dislodged and angled free.

Willow stared, impressed by its size.

"Deer leg," he said. "It may be left from the old time. They say that before the Wave there were many deer. Now the few bones we find on the heath, left by the dogs, are splintered and broken before we pick them up. So the boy must take care with this one."

Willow nodded. Great Mother had spoken of deer hunts, although it was hard to see what she described—so many more huts, so many people.

Seeing didn't come easily to Willow. Sometimes she had an empty feeling when she summoned Great Mother's story voice to recite the hunt: *In the time of plenty, before the Wave demolished the People of the Singing Seals and their homes, grazing herds sometimes came within range of the headland. Then all the people and their dogs spread out around the wild creatures and drove them over the cliff. In the time of plenty there was enough meat and bones and skin and horn for all.*

Too soon now it would be up to Willow to make others see these long-ago ways. If only she could keep doubt from creeping unbidden into her thoughts. Like a furtive mouse it could nibble at the core of Great Mother's tellings until they crumbled into dust. And with Great Mother herself beginning to question the knowledge she had gathered and taught, how was Willow to hold within herself all that the living are meant to carry forward from the past?

Thrusting aside this worry, she turned her attention to Thorn, who would need tending even if he was to manage on his own. It was a task she would gladly hand on to someone else. Why not Hazel or Crab or Thistle?

She lifted the deer leg, which was surprisingly heavy and slippery. She would have to rub off the oily soot that had built up over time. She looked around for a bit of rock-weed or skin.

"You were to make haste," Uncle Redstone reminded her.

She took the deer leg outside, veered away toward the beach, and stooped to wipe the bone on dune grass. Food, she reminded herself. She had meant to bring along something to eat. She started back to the huts.

But Uncle Redstone had just emerged from the passage, and he saw her. All she could do now was turn on her heel and head out to Thorn.

With hunger already gnawing at her, she would prod him into action. Let him make the best of the deer leg and keep up with her across the heath, or he would be sleeping this night on an empty belly.

THORN

Father said I should not fear the unknown. He said that what is new and strange may heal as well as harm. If he could know that I was to be shunned here, what would he tell me of it? I listen for his voice, his words. I try to hear them on the wind.

First, I suppose, he would remind me that he and his mother and father never truly belonged to the people of the High Island. Except my mother. He belonged to her and she to him. So next he would speak of their life together. And her care of me. Then he would bid me dwell on every harmless act since my coming here. That, I think, is how he would have me endure all this.

Well, then. They have sheltered me. They gave me a skin garment. They leave food, and it is enough, although sometimes, like now, I hunger.

Willow says there will be nothing to eat until we reach the appointed place. She sounds angry about it, as if I were to blame. Still, she is here with me. Even though she surges ahead from time to time, she always stops to wait. So there is Willow, who talks to me, who sometimes learns from me, who leads me toward a new unknown but does not abandon me. The bone stick is another gift. I am learning how to plant it forward and lift myself into the next step. Yes, and there is the dog, always the dog. With nothing to eat along the way, he has already sniffed the walking bone up and down.

"How much farther?" I ask her when I pause.

She points to a distant hill.

It looks beyond beyond. I lower myself with care, landing on my strong knee. After a moment I slide sideways, stretch my leg, lean upon my elbow.

She stands over me. "You may not stop. You must keep going."

"In a while," I say, my head dropping down to the heath. I can feel the shrunken leg twitch. I grab it to keep it still.

"Why does it do that?" she asks, staring. She does not laugh or squirm with disgust.

"It happens when the strength is gone," I try to explain.

"You said it could not move," she says. "Now it does."

"But not to my bidding. Not like my real leg and my hands." I wave them one at a time. I bend them, straighten them.

She sits down beside me. I sense that she is weary too and welcomes this rest.

She reaches out to my shrunken leg. She pinches it, and my hand flies out at her, smacking her off. The dog jumps to his feet.

"It feels?" she exclaims in surprise.

"Yes, it does. I do. It is a part of me."

She scowls. "What is the use of it, then?"

"No use. It is what was left after the sickness, the sleep."

She is silent a moment. Then she says, "Thistle thinks your true leg may be left behind on the Last Island. It might yet come. It might catch up."

I cannot speak to this. I do not know where I went that time, where I was before each awakening.

Willow leans forward. She says, "It is partly with you and

partly absent." She spreads her fingers above the grass and with the other hand points to the shadow they make. "Like this." Then, suddenly bold, she declares, "Like the dogs and the seals and the face on the stone. I saw them, Thorn. You left them there."

Here is something else I do not understand. She is not quite angry, but she is disturbed. I try to calm her. I say, "They are nothing. They have no life of their own, no power."

"Such things are not allowed," she tells me. "Never. When sometimes the little children make shadow shapes like that, they are punished. They learn not to make them. Were you never taught this?"

"Not at all. We make shadows on our pots and on our walls. I can show you birds I have not seen here. I can show you—"

"No!" She shouts this at me. "You need to learn our ways," she tells me. "It is not … safe to be so different."

I lie back, chastened, silent. Closing my eyes against the sky's glare, I try to shut out Willow, distance myself from all of them here, everything. I listen for the surrounding sea, but already it is out of my hearing. There is only the wind, the rasping bark of a raven, and a frenzy of small ground birds signaling the coming night.

WILLOW

Willow's thoughts swung between resentment at being held to Thorn's pace and fear that he would collapse and die along the way. Where were the others? Why didn't anyone come looking for her and Thorn? She imagined them around a fire, the shelter completed, a meal of dried fish or birds finished as well. She could smell no food, see no smoke, hear no voices. That could only mean that she and Thorn still had a long way to go.

He kept lagging behind, his head bent forward, his body twisting with each labored step. She couldn't bear to watch him, but she didn't dare lose sight of him.

Then out of her desperation a spark shot up. He needed rest. The dog could stay with him while she ran ahead. It wouldn't take her long to reach the others. They would help.

"It is only to the other side of that hill," she told him. "Do you see?"

Thorn was too breathless to speak.

"Well, of course you cannot see from here, but when you come to the hilltop, you will see down the far slope where stones lie about." She faltered. If she wasn't asking him to continue on his own, he needn't know his destination. He still didn't realize that a shelter was being prepared just for him.

"You may rest here," she said. "Do not wander off." This command was out of her mouth before she knew it.

He sent her a look at once bleak and wry. Wander? the

look seemed to ask. His lips parted, but still he said nothing. The struggle to keep going had sapped his strength.

When Willow left him, he was beginning to settle himself, both his hands reaching to untangle his useless leg from the good one. She started at a run, then slowed, looking back to note any landmarks that would lead her straight to him on her return. But in this direction there wasn't much to fasten on. Never mind, she told herself. The grass she trampled should show her the way. Besides, he wasn't likely to stir before she returned with help.

As soon as the others caught sight of Willow, there was an outcry. Tall Reed, uneasy so far from the settlement, had a dread of this place with its patterns of stone hinting at buried walls. So she was ready to rail at anyone who kept her here.

"You lost him? You lost the boy?" she charged.

Willow said, "Left him. He cannot walk anymore. Maybe some of us should drag him on a sealskin as we do the trees. And he needs to eat. We both do."

"You brought no food?" Outraged, Tall Reed flung out a hand. But instead of striking Willow, she let it drop. "Why Great Mother relies on such a one as you ..." She didn't complete her remark. Still, she had said enough to let Willow understand that whatever food had been brought along had already been consumed.

Willow glanced from Hazel to Thistle to Crab. Crab nodded slightly. Carefully Willow shifted her glance from him, letting it fall on a few small bones from the meal she had missed.

She waited until Tall Reed's back was turned before seeking whatever Crab still held. While Tall Reed retrieved the bed skins from the shelter and spread them out, Willow sidled close to him. His hand slid from inside his loose garment and placed in hers a fistful of bird meat.

"Is this all?" she whispered, fighting the urge to stuff the entire amount into her mouth.

"All," he replied.

She allowed herself one bite. It was dense and salty, so she chewed it a long time before she swallowed. No more, she told herself. She clutched the remaining food so hard it was nearly squeezed out between her fingers.

Tall Reed doubted that the bed skins could support the boy without being torn apart, but Willow could take Crab and try. They went off together, the skins rolled under their arms, with Willow still clutching the last portion of bird meat.

She had no trouble finding Thorn, even though he was lying flat in the grass. The dog, which was leaping and pouncing on some small prey, stopped his hunting to go to the boy and stand beside him.

Thorn sat up. Willow handed over the remnant of bird meat. He hesitated. "Some for you?" he asked.

"For you," she told him, adding, "At least you can speak again."

A trace of his smile returned. "I think I slept," he said.

She and Crab laid out one skin and told Thorn to lie on it. First, though, he had to eat. The dog sat and watched attentively. Thorn pulled a scrap of bird meat from his mouth and held it out to the dog. Without standing, the dog leaned toward the proffered bit and deftly picked it from between Thorn's fingers.

"I would not do that," Crab remarked.

Willow could tell that for him Thorn's trusting gift seemed a foolhardy dare.

The skin they were using to haul Thorn over the heath lasted until they had to climb the hill. As it dragged and began to pull apart, Willow caught hold of Thorn's arm. Even so, Crab couldn't bring himself to touch him. They tried going across the side of the hill instead, but once the skin had begun to give way, it was soon in tatters.

Crab unrolled the other skin. It was in worse condition than the one they had destroyed. He shook his head. "Could you walk from here?" he asked Thorn.

Thorn was willing to try. Reaching for the deer leg, he swiveled and then pulled himself upright. To lessen the steepness Crab led him aslant the hill. By the time they had made their way to a point where they could begin to descend, Thorn was ready to rest again and Crab was ready to try hauling him on the skin. This worked long enough to bring Thorn within reach of the shelter. He made the final approach on foot, under the curious and uneasy gaze of Tall Reed.

She wasted no time. Blunt and brisk, she told Thorn that she and the others should have returned home long since. He would have to make the best of the shelter and its bedding until Willow brought him more provisions, including food. He would find water in a spring among the stones over there. Tall Reed waved in the direction of the buried stones. He must remain in this place until he was sent for.

Thorn's disbelief turned slowly to comprehension. Stricken, he looked around at one and then another of those preparing to leave him. Finally his gaze came to rest on Willow.

At once she realized that she had never finished telling him of Great Mother's plan. She opened her mouth to explain, but no words came. It was too late now to consider how he must feel, so far from the sight and sound of the sea. She had meant all along to prepare him for this. In truth she had meant to. She couldn't think how to say that it had slipped from her thoughts.

Willow awoke to seal singing. Even in her bed closet she could feel dampness seeping into everything. Fog like this could last for days. It could alter everyone's plans. Everyone except Mizzle's unborn baby. That child to come was the only person who could ignore the dripping gray pall that would hang over the settlement and drench the surrounding land.

Willow turned her face to the stone wall and shut her eyes. No need to leave this close warmth, especially after yesterday's strenuous trek.

She heard the crackle of dried rockweed on live embers. She lay very still, listening. If someone placed a fish over the fire, she would be unable to resist its lure. She heard footsteps and muffled voices. She was drifting back into sleep when the unmistakable sound of sputtering flames roused her. She turned toward the hearth, where Bramble tended the fire. Bramble placed a stone slab on it to heat. Someone called, and Bramble let out a sigh of impatience, but she hurried from the hut.

Willow waited. When she was sure the stone slab was ready for cooking, she threw back her cover and slid out of the bed. She took the fish lying ready on the shelf and deposited it carefully onto the heated slab. The instant sizzling produced a gush of steam.

Would this bring Bramble running back? Using two flat shells, Willow flipped the fish onto its raw side. Fresh steam plumed up. And still Bramble did not reappear. No one did.

Willow didn't dare hope that she might be left to herself

with so much food. Every lesson about sharing vanished at this prospect. After all, she had barely eaten yesterday, and she had labored hard for the good of the people.

With one shell she cut off a portion of fish above the tail and scooped it off the slab. This part usually cooked first, but it was still slightly raw. That didn't matter. It soothed the craving inside her. Soon more would be ready, and she would eat her fill. Then, if no one came, she would crawl back inside the bed closet to laze in perfect comfort.

It occurred to her that she might have to answer to Bramble or Father or someone else. How would she explain the eaten fish? She might suggest that a bold seabird could have ventured into the hut and helped itself. She flipped the fish again. She cut another section, but she ate it too quickly, burning her tongue. She reached for a dipper of water and savored the long, cool drink. That made her think of the boy, Thorn, newly arrived and thirsting. She had fetched him water then. She had even tried to comfort him.

This abrupt reminder stopped her cold. Last night she had walked away from him without a word. She had misled him and then left him, and now he was waiting for her, maybe frightened, certainly hungry.

She sprang up, rummaging through cast-off containers until she found a pouch of the right size. Made from the stomach of a large seabird, the pouch had an oily interior that would seal in the fish and all its juices. What else? On her way out, she could take a few dried birds from the pit where they were stored. She might even find some strips of salted seal meat.

While she rushed about, she found herself wondering where Great Mother was. Had she gone on her mysterious quest again?

As Willow made her way along the passage, she heard some kind of commotion from another hut. She halted. But the big wind stone had been dragged across the entrance to that hut, so she continued on.

Out in the gloom she saw no one. Even if people were nearby, they would blend into the background. She listened for voices. From beyond the dunes came the murmur of the sea. It had a pulse of its own. Now it surged, now it curled upon itself, now it hissed. Willow knew its familiar rhythms as well as any story. Only once, when Great Mother was a child, had its constancy failed.

Great Mother had said that when the sea burst beyond its bounds, roaring like a beast enraged, she herself never saw the tremendous wall of water that reared up and hurled itself upon the land and most of the living. If there was warning, it had been ignored. What Great Mother recalled from that time was that the sky had turned yellow and a sour stench had choked the throat and burned the eyes. Did she fear it might happen again? She had not said so. Yet she must wonder, along with others, whether Thorn's arrival was linked to a new upheaval to come.

Willow pondered all of this as she rolled food for Thorn inside her own sealskin bed cover. Great Mother was relying on her to learn any secrets he might disclose, but the people's rejection of his net made her wary. Even if his rope were to be noticed, it was unlikely to fare any better. Then there were those shadow figures. Willow couldn't imagine their effect on the uncles. At least for a while, though, they might be spared discovery. As long as Thorn was held in dread, there was little chance that anyone would step inside the halfwall to enter the corner or even peer into it.

Striding up the slope away from the settlement, Willow heard a sudden clamor of seabirds offshore. Probably a hunting bird was raiding a rookery. Then the raucous flurry subsided and the seals resumed their croon, the hollow voices rising and falling as the animals slipped from offshore rocks and trawled the shallows.

As sometimes happened, dogs responded with a few half-hearted howls. Willow thought she heard an echo far inland, a throaty plaint uttered just once. Was it the one-eared dog connecting with his pack?

Recalling the likeness of that dog on the stone in Thorn's corner, Willow was struck by the thought that the shadow shapes might somehow reveal the mystery of Thorn. He had assured her that they had no life of their own. Yet she wasn't fully convinced. If they did possess the power of his making, could they also determine his fate?

So far only she and Thorn knew about them. That knowledge might be an advantage. But in what way? She had no idea whether the advantage lay in telling or in holding back.

Shifting the weight of her load, she trudged on.

Inland the fog thinned. A trace of brightness from above made the sodden grass and flowers glisten. Willow's heart lifted. After yesterday, it felt good to set her own pace and to reaffirm how easily she could cover the distance.

"You're not very far away," she told Thorn when she found him sitting on a stone with various pulled weeds at hand. The dog was nowhere in sight.

He looked up at her but didn't respond.

"I brought fish straight from the fire," she informed him. "In a good stomach pouch you can use afterward."

His look didn't waver.

She noticed that he was wearing the skin garment over his tunic. It hadn't occurred to her that he might be cold. She ought to have brought him some live embers as well. But what could he use for fuel? "Is it warm inside the shelter?" she asked him.

"Warmer than outside," he replied tonelessly.

"So why not go in?" she demanded, beginning to feel that he was blaming her for his discomfort as well as his solitude.

"It is dark," he said. "There is no space."

She glanced at the shelter, a slipshod construction of bones askew and skins barely covering them, with none of them fastened. "It's only for a little while," she told him, hoping that a strong wind wouldn't blow it down before he was released.

His level gaze was unnerving, his silence accusing. Had she used those very words to reassure him in order to bring him here? Something like that, she supposed.

She knelt down and opened the skin wrappings. "Here," she said with forced brightness as she handed him the pouch with the fish. "This should fill you up for now, and there is more. Much more. You will not be hungry again, and I shall come with another load. As soon as you need it. Even before that."

She couldn't stop this onrush of promises. If only he would speak. If only he would seize the fish and devour it. "Tell me what else you want here," she blurted. She knew she should be careful of what she offered. But the words kept tumbling out of her, words that did nothing to fill the chasm that separated her from Thorn.

She kept busy until there was nothing more to do or say. Then she sat down on the sopping grass across from the bundles of weeds.

The dog came loping up from the stone place, sniffed at the fish in Thorn's hands, and then went a little way off and flopped on his side. Thorn picked off a sizable chunk of fish and placed it on the ground. The dog eyed it but didn't stir. When Thorn began to eat from the pouch, the dog rose, walked to the fish on the ground, swallowed it in a single gulp, and returned to his resting place.

Willow had never seen a dog with such restraint. Only the injured or dying refrained from grabbing whatever they could snatch. The pack could be beaten off, but seldom without losses or damage to supplies. That was why food was stored underground or high up out of dogs' reach. Yet here the dried birds and strips of seal meat lay upon the skin, exposed but untouched.

She glanced at the weeds Thorn had gathered. What was he making now?

If Thorn was ravenous, he didn't show it. He took small bites and chewed slowly before swallowing each mouthful. Then when only a part of the fish was consumed, he closed the pouch and dropped it onto the skin. Leaning forward without rising, he folded all the food inside it and used the deer leg to shove the packet into the shelter's opening.

After that he held his hands out to the dog, which came forward and licked them clean. Then he picked up the weeds he had been twining and resumed his work. First he fixed the knotted end of the fibers around his toes and straightened his leg. Then he leaned back to increase the length between his foot and his hands.

"I can hold the end for you," Willow finally suggested. "Would that help?"

He nodded.

Willow hesitated. Was his assent agreement that it would or acceptance that she could?

When he made no further gesture of accommodation, Willow shimmied sideways until she was facing him and could lift the anchored end from his toes. She noticed now that his end was attached to a small bone that he twirled. This was different from braiding split fibers, but it seemed to have a similar effect. After watching for a while, she couldn't stop herself from asking him what he was making.

"A rope," he said.

"A rope from weeds?"

He nodded.

She looked at the braided rope that held his pouch. "What is it for?" she asked.

"It can be used in many ways," he told her without offering a fuller explanation.

She let out a sigh of exasperation, which he ignored. "I will have to go back in a while," she declared.

He didn't even look up.

"I was going to tell you more about coming here," she finally blurted. "But you were so tired. You went to sleep. The sun was going into the sea, and I had to have you here before dark." She fell silent.

He added fresh weeds as he twisted the rope in progress. The length between them was becoming limp, so Willow scrambled backward to keep it taut. Without realizing it, she bumped the sleeping dog, and he raised his head. Instinctively she recoiled, unable to quell a shudder, a tightening in her throat. But the strain from contact was all in her, not in the dog, who shifted his hindquarters to the side and paid her no further heed.

Had Thorn noticed, or was all his attention on the rope-making? She looked down at her whitened knuckles. She should be mindful that this dog was under Thorn's spell. There was no telling how long its meekness would last or whether it might extend to her when she was away from Thorn. She mustn't let down her guard. Maybe Thorn was unaware that the dogs on the outskirts of the settlement weren't tame like those on the High Island.

Or maybe he didn't care.

Before Willow was halfway home, Great Mother, wisps of white hair tangled about her face, emerged out of the fog. "Alone again?" she exclaimed. "Have I not warned you of such folly?"

"I was with the boy," Willow replied. "I brought him food and a sleeping cover. You told me to deal with him."

"Did I? I suppose I did." For a moment Great Mother sounded uncertain. Then she recovered her voice of authority. "Have Crab and Thistle join you next time. If they stay with you until you approach the boy …" Her words trailed off. "Anyway, this waiting will end soon. Mizzle's baby was born alive. A girl."

A girl! A girl to make everyone glad. What did this birth mean for Thorn? "May the boy return now?" Willow asked.

"Not yet. The moon is waning. It is the wrong time to begin a new life. And after those babies born with their back-bones showing, we need to know that there is not some similar flaw beneath the skin of this one."

"How can you look for an unseen flaw?" Willow demanded.

Great Mother sighed. "That is the worry that gnaws at our people. Time may tell. If the baby thrives, maybe they will be able to set aside their fears. But they recall that Thorn's father said he was born whole, the flaw delayed. Just now the men are in turmoil, at odds among themselves. Some think this birth time signifies nature wronged. They say that we can set it right only by ridding ourselves of the twisted boy who was thrust into our midst. Others, including your father, think we cannot rely on the birth time alone to determine what follows. Wait for the new moon, they urge. More may be revealed. I think this view will prevail."

Willow said, "Did they not turn to you for counsel?"

Great Mother brushed back tendrils of fog-drenched hair. "They were not eager to hear from me," she said wryly. "But they did. I had not slept, so I was slow of speech. I reminded them that naming was another beginning and that the child could not be named until the moon waxed toward fullness. I warned them that if they killed the boy now, they would never know the truth about him. That is all I said," she concluded. "I pleaded for time. I spoke for the new moon."

"How many days?" asked Willow.

"We are not halfway through the waning. When the fog lifts and we can see the moon again, then we will know."

"Thorn must stay out there all that time?"

Great Mother spread the fingers of both her hands. "It is no more than this many days, maybe less."

"Am I to tend him still?"

"You are. Although I will speak with him myself. The past keeps rising to the surface with questions anew for the boy."

Willow was tempted to follow Great Mother back to the hillside. But the old woman could sense this and forestalled her. "Go to the others now. Keep away from Mizzle's hut. Be useful and do not draw attention to yourself."

Was she telling Willow not to stir up trouble? Willow supposed so. She watched the bent figure striding off with surprising vigor. Yet a chill crept up Willow's back, a feeling that as the moon waned, so did Great Mother's strength.

Willow continued on her way. She could hear the settlement before she was able to see it, for the fog was still thick along the coast. First there were the high-pitched voices of the younger children. Next came snarling, the start of a dog fight that prompted her to veer away from that direction. Then she recognized Thistle's shout followed by a yelp. She guessed that someone had thrown a stone at the dogs to break up a confrontation.

Coming upon Thistle behind the shell heap, she told him what Great Mother had said about his going with her the next time she brought food to Thorn. Thistle picked up a stone and hurled it at the dogs, who retreated. The stone fell short of its mark.

"They stopped," Willow said. "You should not do that once they are quiet."

Thistle reached down for another stone.

"You could hit one of the children," she pointed out.

"I need to strengthen my throwing arm," he told her.

Crab joined them. "You should use bigger stones," he said.

"For what?" Willow demanded. Were they going on a hunt without her? "It is not the season for seals." But she shouldn't have to point this out. Everyone knew that the singing seals bore their young at the onset of frost. Even when an early snowfall covered the outer ledges and blurred the sightings of white newborn seal pups, children old enough to take to the tree-boats helped drive seal mothers into the water, leaving the pups unprotected. In spite of Tall Reed's objections, Willow had been included in the last seal hunt, and she was determined not to be left out of the next one.

"For the boy," Thistle told her.

"If they decide to," Crab added. "There may be no stoning, no drowning. It is not yet decided."

"It will happen," Thistle said. "It will. They will drive him into the sea with stones. That is how it can be done without touching him."

"Or they might decide to send him from here in a tree-boat," said Crab.

Thistle's voice rose. "My father says that only stoning or drowning can right the wrong of him."

Willow swallowed a retort. If Thistle had been present when the men gathered to consider the birth, he must have missed Great Mother's counsel. Or had his father rejected her advice?

Willow glanced from one boy to the other. Thistle looked agitated; Crab looked anxious. Avoiding the matter of Thorn, she asked whether they had seen the baby.

"Only women were there," said Crab. "Mizzle screamed."

Thistle said, "How could you not hear her? Where were you?"

"Tending the boy," Willow said.

It was their turn to stare at her. Did she detect a flicker of fear in Thistle's eyes? Wariness and excitement mingled in Crab's expression.

Let them dwell on what she had told them, she thought. Then, just before she walked off, she informed them that in the next few days they would be expected to join her when she brought food to the boy. "Only you need not come close," she informed them loftily. "I will go all the way."

THORN

I understand now. Solitude is not so terrible. What makes this banishment hard is false hope. I believed Willow. I believe her no longer. I must do what I can for myself whether or not she returns.

After she left the second time, the old woman came. She sat across from me as Willow had done and watched me for a while. Finally she spoke. "Have you enough to eat?" she asked. I said I had. Then she said, "I must ask again: Who are you?"

"My father told your people. What he said is all I know."

She plucked a bud from one of the weeds I had prepared and held it in her open hand. Her fingers are thin and bent, the joints swollen, the skin like a baby bird's. Can she see that my shrunken leg and her hands have something in common? She did not look at her hands or at my leg, though. She looked into my eyes.

"You may be … sent away," she told me.

I suppose she meant I would be given to the sea. But as long as I do not speak aloud of this deed, maybe it will keep its distance and allow me to prepare.

"You … we have a little time left. I think you can tell me more than you think you know. Here are some of the questions that my people are asking. If you are one of us, why do you look so different? Beyond the difference of the leg. Lately we have had newborn babies shaped even more strangely."

I tried to tell her I was not always like this. "Before the sickness, the long sleep, I ran and climbed and jumped. That was before the leg withered like a plucked weed. Since that happened, the leg has marked me as ill-favored."

"Even if your leg were whole," she said, "there is your small size, your dark hair."

"I look more like my mother than my father. When the boat brought me here, the difference should have been plain to see. There was my father, like your men. There were the others, all of my mother's people."

"I was not here," she said, rocking a little, opening and closing her fingers. "I did not see them. Even though I know more than those who did, I still do not know enough." She was watching me as she spoke. She said, "There is strength in your hands, there is power in your craft. Where does this come from?"

I had no answer. But something in her manner gave me the strength to speak the unspeakable. "If I am to be sent into the sea," I asked, "might they let me go in a boat of my own making?"

She seemed startled by the turn I had taken. Had she sensed my dread when I flung out my question? "I had not thought …" she said. "But how could you?"

I wondered if she meant that no boat could save me. I said, "I think it would be fitting to leave as I came." These words arose of their own accord, informing me as well as her.

She frowned, stretched out her scrawny arms, and let them fall on her knees. After a moment she said, "It is not yet certain that you must go. I am here to learn what I can. Your father told my people that his mother and father were plucked from an offshore rock near this coast and carried to safety in a winged boat from a distant land. He said it happened during a great upheaval of the sea. But no boat could have held against the wave that overcame the People of the Singing Seals. It swept away almost everyone and all that had belonged to them."

"This is what I know," I replied. "My father's mother and father were taking birds. Then the sky changed color. The sea was sucked away. They saw the bottom. My father's father tied them both high up at the top. The rope held fast."

"The top!" the old woman exclaimed. "The top of what?"

"The tallest rock, I suppose. My father's mother said they were stranded there for days before the boat took them off. Their home was gone. The land itself was gone. The sea rose so that they were no longer high above it, the water full of all manner of things—trees and bloated beasts and even dead kinsmen. That is what she told me."

"Taking birds," the old woman said. "High above the sea. On top of the stack?"

All I could tell her was that my father knew of the stack from his mother and father. He looked for it as we followed the coastline in search of the homeland. I said, "Two times we were close to offshore stacks that might have been the landmark my father sought, for we could see the likes of broken dwellings, too. When at last we came to the great tall stack beyond your beach, he gave a shout. He seemed to recognize it from all that his mother and father had ever told him. And then to find people here as well! He was overjoyed."

I had spoken more fully than I had intended. But I could feel the old woman's hunger for understanding. Deep in thought, she shook her head and shook it again. Finally she spoke. "Have you said this to Willow?"

"I say little to her."

"She should be told," the old woman muttered, struggling to her feet. "She needs to hear anything that helps to fill the gaps in our story."

I must guard against thoughts that ought not be spoken, for I nearly said aloud that if it mattered that much to the old woman, she should tell Willow herself. When I am alone like this, the distinction between thought and speech fades. As I come to understand that I will never make a place for myself with the People of the Singing Seals, the world closes in around me, and my choices dwindle.

These musings held me awhile. Then, gradually, I became aware of the old woman standing over me.

"You asked for something before, and now it has leaked from my thoughts," she said.

I looked up at her. I said, "A boat of my making."

"Yes," she said. "That was it. You should begin to build it soon, even if you never have to use it."

"I will need things," I said.

She straightened for an instant. Then her body sagged. "I will try not to lose all you have said to me. Tell Willow what you need." She started to leave and then turned. "There may be power in your crafting, but I do not think you are one of the Boundless from the Last Island." She was frowning. "We are nearly finished, we People of the Singing Seals. You might have mattered here, but I think it is too late."

After she walked away, the dog crawled out of the shelter. He stretched and yawned. He sniffed the place where she had been. Then he trotted down to the stones, probably to hunt the mice and voles that burrow there.

WILLOW

Hazel's voice reached Willow as she crouched in the shallows scraping limpets from rocks. She had followed the curving shore toward the point that tailed off into deeper water. When the tide was low, she could find weed-capped rocks here, and their sturdy crop of shellfish. At her coming, sheep had clattered away from their browsing and splashed out toward the ledges. So she was alone now, blissfully alone. After nearly two fogbound days full of chatter about Mizzle's baby, all she wanted was to get away by herself to think.

Ignoring Hazel's call, she continued to pry off the tiny shellfish, which she dropped into a skin container. Despite the scraper's dulled edge, she had put off returning to the hut for a sharpening stone. This allowed her to preserve her solitude.

"Willow!" Hazel was closer now.

Willow squatted, nearly doubled over, all but her shoulders and head immersed. If the fog didn't conceal her, maybe it would give her the look of one more boulder among the others.

Hazel's pursuit distracted her, scrambling her thoughts. She stared at her feet. Through the water they appeared magnified and distorted. What if they never recovered their true shape? How would it feel to stumble up to the settlement on bulbous stumps? Who would be the first to notice, to alert the uncles and her father? Who would speak of nature gone awry and who of stoning? Who would drive her into the sea?

At last Hazel moved off. As soon as her voice faded, Willow straightened. By now she was chilled to the bone. Shivering, she splashed shoreward and set her container down on the sand. For all her efforts it held a scant harvest of limpets. Clutching herself, she rubbed her arms and hopped from one foot to the other. She looked down. There they were, her feet, with no disfigurement, except that they had turned a mottled blue.

Glancing up at the dismal sky, she beheld a trace of the sun, a fuzzy disc of light. If only it would break through. All she needed was a hint of warmth to stiffen her resolve to fill her container to the brim. At the least she should fill the container halfway before emptying it into a keeping vat to soak.

Back to scraping, she waited for her disconnected thoughts to surface. As if caught in fretful eddies, they swirled around each other: new moon and new life, strange boat and stranger boy with shrunken leg, misshapen feet, and … Not feet, she commanded her bobbing thoughts. She had done with feet. Still, the thought of them refused to depart. Feet, then.

Willow halted, scraper poised. In spite of the water's way of tricking her eyes, she knew her feet were as they should be.

Up from the recent past floated a recollection of another birth. That life had been so brief that for Willow it was easily dismissed. The infant, born with a misshapen foot, had been swiftly dealt with. After that, two—no, three—anxiously awaited births before Mizzle's, and only one child still alive.

Now there was Mizzle's baby, a girl, unflawed. But even with an unflawed back and full hands and feet, her birth couldn't quell the people's misgivings. Where did Thorn fit into this scheme? Why was he both threat and promise? How could one maimed boy hold such power?

Willow glanced into the container. Not yet full enough. Her arms ached from pressing so hard with the dulled scraper. She wondered what this tiresome task would feel like with Thorn's sharp fire stone in her hand. The next time she brought food to him she might ask to try it. Or was it possible to take it without his knowing? This thought brought a shiver of excitement, and that in turn made her realize she was no longer cold.

She noticed a faint shadow leaning from her body. It seemed about to tip over into the water. That gave her pause. Could it mean more than that the sun was beginning to burn through the fog? Unlike the shadow beasts on the stone that she couldn't blot out, her shadow wouldn't remain in the water after she gained the beach. Or would it? How could she tell unless she was there to look? And if she was there again, so would it be. But tipping into the sea? That might be Thorn's fate to come, but was it to be hers as well? That disturbing question clung to her as she headed for the shore.

By the time she was back in the hut and had dumped the limpets in the vat to soak, her only thought was to avoid Tall Reed, who was always ready to send her to some new, disagreeable task. She was tempted to go fishing with Thorn's net, but it was too soon to use the limpets for bait. They wouldn't lure the fish until they swelled and softened.

As she made her way out through the passage, she saw that the wind stone still blocked the doorway into Mizzle's hut. Outside she glanced into the work place, which looked deserted. The entire settlement was curiously empty.

Where had everyone gone? What event was she missing now?

She climbed the shell heap and looked around. She still

couldn't see very far, but at least she ought to hear the children. Nothing. Then she caught sight of old Gray Cloud shuffling toward her.

"Where did they go?" she called to him.

"To the trees," he said.

"All of them?"

"All."

"No one said," she responded, aggrieved. "How long since?" She could catch up with the slow ones.

The only thing he said was, "Dogs out there." Warning her.

She should have been elated to be left like this, free for a while. But all she could think of was what she might miss. First bird-hunting on the stack, now a journey to the trees. If they found a deer there, they would try to bring it down. Without her.

She wandered into the work place to look for a sharpening stone. She saw that part of the corner halfwall had been pulled aside and one of its stones put to another use. It was lying flat on supports and was strewn with flakes from axe-making. She brushed them from the surface. A few marks showed, but nothing that could be recognized as part of a figure.

She went to the space where the stone had been propped on edge and looked into Thorn's corner. Stepping through the gap, she turned to face what remained of the halfwall. The skins and Thorn's net were undisturbed. But sooner or later someone would reach over to grab a skin from that pile. Then the shadow shapes on the inner facing of the stone would be exposed.

She sank back on her heels, seeing the animals anew and

finding other lines that hinted at a dappled sea. The seals together presented a vision of an entire world. The dogs were grouped apart from them but connected with one another. Only the face and the one-eared dog appeared separate. The dog, unfinished, seemed closer. Amazement welled up in her at the mystery of what Thorn had brought to life. Yet he maintained that they had no power of their own, and now Great Mother doubted that shadow figures detached from beasts could do as they willed, free and untouchable. Willow was baffled. What, then, were these shadow shapes that held her in thrall? She had to blink back tears, knowing that they were bound to be discovered and destroyed.

Willow found Thorn in the wetland beyond the buried stones. He was wading among the reeds. The dog was swimming in the marsh.

"There you are," she called to him, sounding glad to see him. Well, she *was* glad. When she hadn't found him at the shelter, her first thought had been that he, too, had deserted her. "I brought fire as well as food," she told him.

He came coated with mud and bearing an armful of reeds. The deer leg kept sticking whenever he drove it down for support. She thought about taking the reeds for him, leaving him two hands to deal with the stick. But she was reluctant to descend into that mire. She even backed away a bit as he approached.

"They all went to get trees," she said, watching him struggle to keep his balance. "Almost all of them."

"Not you," he replied as he paused to rest.

"I did not know. I was gathering bait. They left without me." She didn't say that she had deliberately ignored Hazel, who must have been sent to bring her along. Then she caught a look in Thorn's eyes that sent a chill through her. Suddenly it came to her that she had been complaining about missing out on the journey to the trees. Complaining to him who had been left on his own in this desolate place.

Once Thorn was on solid ground, she took the reeds from him and carried them up the slope. She had already started a small fire from the embers she had brought. Thorn went straight to it and stood as close as he could without getting burned. Only now did it occur to her that he might welcome a stone pot for heating food.

When she started to unwrap the seal strips, his raised hand stopped her. "Fresh meat first," he said. "The dried kind will keep."

Without benefit of the deer leg he hobbled into the shelter. When he emerged, he had two plucked ducks. Using discarded bones to prop them over the flames, he set them to cook.

She felt a twinge of envy. "How did you get them?" she asked.

"The dog," he told her. "I took eggs. He took the birds."

After a while the ducks got hot enough to ooze their oily juices. The flame sputtered and crackled, nearly went out, and then sprang up more wildly than before.

She said, "If you leave the feathers on, they catch fire at once and the cooking does not take so long."

"If I you leave the feathers on," he replied, "they burn."

"That is what I am saying," she told him.

"And I am saying I may have need of feathers. I keep them."

She waited for him to tell her how they might be used,

but he spoke no more of feathers. He busied himself with the cooking, turning both fowls. The fire responded with renewed energy, and the aroma lulled her into a state of quiet bliss.

The dog appeared, his fur spiked with mud. He stretched out near the fire, his muzzle resting on his forepaws, his eyes fastened on Thorn.

Only when Thorn flipped the ducks off the fire and onto the ground did the dog's gaze shift from him to the food. After one of them had cooled a little, Thorn divided it into three portions. The dog gulped his down, trotted off to a safe distance, coughed it all out onto the ground, and, crouching over it, started to tear and chew in earnest.

Thorn and Willow ate in silence. Finally, just as Willow started to crunch a bone for the marrow, he asked her not to.

"You can use these bones?" she asked with surprise. "They have little strength."

"They are hollow," he said. "They are light." He nodded toward the dog. "Only that one cannot be stopped."

She glanced over at the dog, now rolling on the greasy patch left from his meal. "In the old days," she said, "before the Wave, the dogs understood all the people's words. They did their bidding."

He said, "They could still learn to work for you."

Willow shook her head. "No, the good ones all drowned. These are from the wild. They understand only what they fear."

He said nothing, but his look disputed her claim.

"Well, maybe this one is different," she admitted grudgingly.

"He was here before I came," Thorn said. "Your people ignore what is in the dogs and the seals. If they watched and listened, they might connect with the beasts."

"You have skills ..." She groped for words to express her thoughts. "If we could learn ..." But she was about to speak of a time that might never come for him.

He said, "I will be gone from here before long."

He knew! Was he able to see into the day after tomorrow and the day after that? She said, "Nothing is certain until the old moon passes and the new moon begins."

"My father crafted the boat that brought me here," he continued. "I will craft another for going away. It need not be as large and strong as his, for its load will be lighter."

"It might not be needed," she insisted.

"Will you fetch me things?" he asked.

"You might stay!"

He didn't try to explain or justify his urgency. Instead he said, "Rib bones and skins and whale fat and seal guts. One straight tree. The stomachs of the great sharp-beaked diving birds with yellow heads. Their oil must be saved, though it will not be applied to the skin cover until the boat is almost ready for the sea."

While her mind registered what he required, it floundered in the face of his determination. "Diving birds?" she mumbled helplessly.

"Those with the black lines along the cheeks. Their feathered wings as well."

"They do not come ashore," she said.

"Take them at night. Out where they nest. The ledges may be seen in the dark because of their white droppings."

"I have been forbidden to bird-hunt on the stack."

"They roost on the outer ledges. I have seen them off the headland."

She thought a moment. If she dragged a tree-boat into

the shallows, she could row out there this night while almost everyone was gone. But could she take the birds alone? What if the boat slipped away and left her stranded? She must not let this happen. After all, it was to be her hunt. She would not fail.

She jumped up, ready to set off at a run.

"Wait," he said. "The rope I made is behind the shelter. Take it. It is longer and tougher than the ropes I have seen on the tree-boats."

At the back she spotted the coiled rope among bundled reeds. What else was he making with them? She picked up the rope and started off.

"Wait," he said again. "The rope. I must have it back."

She turned and looked at him. She said, "I am surprised you would let me use it."

"It will help," he said.

"So would the fire stone." The words burst out of her.

He sucked in his breath and eyed her. Then he said, "You would cut yourself."

"I would not," she retorted. "I only want to try ... to feel it in my hand."

He fumbled in his pouch and brought out the shiny black stone. "In the right hands this can do all manner of things. Yes, even make a quick and silent kill. But if you took it to the bird ledge, it would likely slip from your grasp before you could strike. The sea would keep it."

He was speaking to her as elders speak to children. She wished she hadn't mentioned that stone. Now he was aware of her fascination with it, her longing. Maybe the stone itself possessed that knowledge, giving him its power over her.

Turning away, she hooked the rope over her arm.

"Before you go," he said, "you may hold this for a little time."

She whipped around, then halted. Was this some kind of trick? Would he allow her a moment with the stone so that he could flaunt what he had and she had not? If only she could resist. She would rather leave the impression that her craving was little more than a passing fancy.

But the moment he held up the stone to her, her steps slowed. She kept her hands at her sides until she was kneeling in front of him. The rope slid onto the ground. She felt the smooth surface of the stone in her palm, the perfect, deadly edge. She felt its power and his craftiness. His resolve.

To Willow's dismay, Crab and Thistle appeared during the lingering twilight. They had been sent back to help her, they said.

"But who sent you?" she demanded. "Tall Reed? What does she think—"

"It was Great Mother," said Thistle. "She met us partway out, but we had to go on until we could hand over our packs to others."

"She had me return with mine," Crab told her. "It has two of the big skins. I told her they are for dragging trees and that the uncles will be angry. She did not care about the uncles."

Willow supposed she could put the boys to work collecting things. But how could she manage to keep them from her bird hunt? She noted their sweat marks, the way they leaned or sat where they could. They must have walked a long distance already. If she kept them moving, they'd be ready to crawl into their bed closets when dark finally came and be deep in sleep by the time she set off for the rookery.

But they questioned all of her bidding.

"Why rib bones? They are for roofing. Are we allowed to take them?"

"These are the best skins. They were saved."

"We have eaten nothing since dawn."

"We need water."

Explaining as little as she could, she decided to tell them about Thorn's boat. After all, they would learn about it when they carried what they collected to his hillside. But as soon as she mentioned the project, the boys rebelled.

"Boats are heavy," said Crab. "Whoever heard of crafting one so far from the sea?"

She hadn't considered that aspect of Thorn's plan. All she could say was, "He has power."

"Power?" Thistle laughed. "When we drive him into the sea, will the boat answer his call and swim over the dry ground to save him?"

"You know it is not yet certain," Willow retorted. "When I was in the passage earlier, I could hear Mizzle's baby squalling. Each day she lives brings us closer to the new moon."

"Still," Crab argued, "this errand makes fools of us."

"It is Great Mother's bidding as well," Willow declared.

But as soon as she said this, she felt uneasy. When Great Mother made the boys turn back, how did she know that Willow would need help bringing Thorn what he required?

"What did she say to you when she sent you to me?" Willow asked.

The boys exchanged glances.

"That we were most needed here," mumbled Crab.

"That we should heed you." Thistle's words fell away.

Willow knew she had to raise the spirits of these two glum

boys. But as long as they drooped with fatigue, she doubted she could arouse their interest. So she told them to refresh themselves with food and drink and then rest awhile.

She watched them slouch off. She supposed that sharing this hunt with them was the best way to bring them to her side. She resented giving in to them, though. This was to have been her foray in the dark of night. Besides, she couldn't forget that when they went off to climb the stack, they had left her behind without a backward glance. Even worse, afterward they had bragged to her about their prowess, their narrow escapes.

She put off the decision for a while. The boys might fall asleep as they rested. She could let that determine whether to include them. Meanwhile she foraged through the bone heap and uncovered a few pieces that might suit Thorn. By true dark, she heard nothing from inside the huts except for Gray Cloud's occasional coughing. Even Mizzle's baby slept.

After fetching Thorn's rope, she made her way to the landing beach. The tree-boats lay side by side above the high-tide line. She chose the one nearest her and started to pull it toward the water. At first it wouldn't budge. Then, when she yanked with all her strength, it yielded a bit. She yanked again. She tried to ease the landward end from the sand. She was able to swivel the boat sideways, but that just aimed it into the boat beside it.

She kept on struggling, fore and aft, before finally admitting defeat. She had to stop and regain her breath before she charged back over the dunes and up to the settlement. In the passage she paused, listening for signs of wakeful boys. Then she made her way into Thistle's hut, where she found him sprawled beside the hearth.

She didn't disturb him. Of the two, he was the one who relished the prospect of stoning Thorn. So she went across the passage in search of Crab, who was curled up inside his bed closet. When she shook him awake, he sat bolt upright, banging his head on the low stone roof.

"What?" he cried.

"Shh," she warned. "Do not wake anyone."

"You woke me," he said.

"So you would not miss the quest. We are going to the rookery. It is arranged."

Slowly he swung his legs around to the floor. Leaning forward, he rubbed his eyes and yawned. "Now?"

"Now, while the diving birds sleep. I will tell you about it after the kill. Until then we have to be so quiet." It just occurred to her that she had forgotten oars.

"I need to pee."

"And I have to get something. So meet me at the tree-boats. Make haste."

She ran along the passageway, her arms spread wide to touch the walls as she felt her way. Outside she groped for oars propped against the work place. If she expected to stay in charge, she must not forget anything else. Still, she had a moment of panic. Where was the rope? The panic subsided. She was certain she had dropped the rope beside the boat.

Once she began to plow through dune grass, she had to hold the oars up higher to keep them from snagging, from tripping her. At last she felt the sand flatten out and then the crackle of dead rockweed and kelp beneath her feet. Now she could follow the tidal debris to the boats.

While she waited for Crab, she decided to tie Thorn's rope to the loop on the tree-boat she had already managed to shift. Her rope for now. Her boat.

She was standing beside it when Crab came down from

the dunes. He had known exactly where to head. Her grip on the rope tightened. Without a word spoken, she would show him she was in control of this tree-boat.

It wasn't until he leaned over to lift it free of the sand that she saw he wasn't alone. Coming down silently behind him, Thistle crossed to the far side of the tree-boat midway along its length.

Willow managed to choke back the cry of dismay that rose up in her. Then she realized that Crab hadn't undermined her plan on purpose. Naturally he assumed that Thistle was to be included. She had been the devious one, trying to make Crab sneak away without waking Thistle.

Facing each other, the boys hoisted the tree-boat and scooted it onto the packed sand. Willow scrambled to grab the forward end, but the dropped rope snagged her ankles and tripped her. By the time she was on her feet again, the boys were shoving the boat into the water.

Willow handed one oar to Crab, but she refused to give up the other one. Thistle would have to do without. Having pushed the boat into deep enough water to prevent its grounding under their weight, they all scrambled on at the same time. Thistle, with both hands free, shoved Willow back and secured a position for himself at the front.

"Give me the oar," he said.

"Shh!" Willow hissed at him. "Not a sound."

It was awkward to paddle from the middle of the long wooden boat, with Crab just behind her. But the night's calm helped, and soon they made headway.

As they drew close to the rookery, she could hear the sleepy mutter of masses of diving birds. But she also heard the strokes of the oars. Choppy water and breaking waves would have covered this sound. Would it alarm the roosting birds?

"Shh," she whispered over her shoulder to Crab, who had not spoken. He seemed to understand, though. He took even greater care to soften the strokes of his oar.

Facing forward again, Willow skipped a stroke to time hers to match his. She stared ahead at blackness, then down at the sparkling phosphorescence stirred by her oar. Where did that light come from? Was the sea full of tiny stars like those in the sky? Or did flames beneath the sea shoot up sparks the way they spewed forth shiny black fire stones from deep within the ground?

All at once a smudge of whiteness spread across their path. Both Willow and Crab checked their strokes, pressing down against the forward motion of the boat. They could feel it bump against a ledge. Rockweed and bird droppings cushioned the sound.

Not the slightest whisper now. Thistle, unencumbered by an oar, was the only one in position to gain the ledge. Willow couldn't prevent him from taking charge. Sliding onto the rock, he kicked the boat off. Willow and Crab brought it close again.

Thistle knew enough to flatten himself and slither as he approached each bird. Willow strained to track his progress, but he was lost to sight. A sigh escaped her. She knew that even if she could have launched the boat by herself, it would have been almost impossible to reach the ledge and secure the boat without alarming the birds.

A strangled squawk broke the silence and was extinguished. It set off a clamor, shrill cries and beating wings, followed by a grunt drawn to a muffled gasp. Willow grabbed a fistful of rockweed so that she could haul herself onto the ledge. She crouched low as she felt her way forward, but almost at once Thistle blocked her.

"Get back," he ordered. "They're attacking. I can't fend them off."

"I have the oar. How many did you kill?"

"Four, maybe five. Swing the oar above me while I collect them."

A moment later he began to hurl the huge dead birds in her direction. She could either catch the ones he flung at her or fight off the attackers, but she couldn't do both at once. She heard a splash.

"Quick!" he said. "Here. Aah! Here! Here!" Now he was rolling over and over toward her, toward the boat. Behind him the avenging birds were already beginning to settle down, their shrillness subsiding. She lowered the oar and gathered the last of the dead birds. Thistle, slimy from head to toe, scrambled past her.

"You must have taken one with a live chick." She didn't bother to hide her contempt. She knew how Thistle's readiness to kill could lead to carelessness.

"How could I tell? All I saw were the white feathers of the big ones."

Willow would have felt beneath the roosting birds, which she had learned to do in utter silence when taking eggs.

"I fetched up one bird from the water," said Crab. "We have six. A good hunt."

A hunt that should have been hers, thought Willow.

But after she had endured the stench of Thistle and was finally able to see his bloodied head and face and arms, she admitted to herself that Crab might have spoken the truth.

THORN

The dog hunts around and under the stones. He has revealed what looks like a settlement in the ground. There are hollows, walls, bones, and tools. As soon as I shifted some of the stones he loosened, he began to disappear into a passageway where voles seem plentiful.

I wonder what else lies there. I am tempted to burrow with the dog, but the boat must come before anything else. I do not know how long I have, and there is much to be done.

Some of the bones that are already tools are like those we use on the High Island. They are gifts from this sandy soil. How is it that they lie among the stones and yet are unknown to the People of the Singing Seals?

Father's sealskin boat was framed with whalebone. Lacking what he used forces me to fashion a vessel similar in appearance, only with different materials. There is no way to know in advance whether it will work, and yet I believe it might. Still, the cleverest crafting will amount to little unless Willow provides me with all I need.

I must have lengths and lengths of fine string, and strong rope, too. If Willow returns before long, maybe she will help with the braiding and plying.

I have come to care about nothing but the making of the boat. I am content in the task until, of a sudden, I stumble onto another gift from underground. Then for a while it holds me spellbound.

This day the dog brought forth a bone teeming with shadow beasts and shadow people. It lifted me. I felt as though I could stand upright, straight and tall.

Willow said her people fear such shadow shapes. I cannot tell what they would make of this bone, so I will hide it and carry it with me onto the sea. Maybe it is a sign for me to make more shadow beasts. Only how would I conceal them here?

I wonder what has become of those I left in the work place, those that Willow saw and railed against. Yet she seemed not to fear them, at least not for herself.

WILLOW

Great Mother returned in advance of the others and helped prepare the birds. She didn't seem surprised to learn that Thorn wanted the stomachs whole but clean. She simply nodded when Willow mentioned that he asked that the stomach oil from the birds be saved for later. Still, when Willow said that he also required the wings, Great Mother frowned in puzzlement, although she offered no objection to including them in the packs.

Great Mother's insight was a mystery to Willow. There was so much she didn't grasp. Was Thorn's crafting skill akin to Great Mother's power to interpret their world? How were power and craftiness gained? Willow was quite sure that she herself possessed neither. So how could she ever take Great Mother's place?

Great Mother made a feast of the fresh bird meat. Then, while Willow and the boys and Gray Cloud ate themselves into a stupor, Great Mother took her portion along with Mizzle's into the closed hut. Later, when she rejoined them, her steps were lively, her eyes bright with hope. Willow had no trouble guessing that the baby continued to thrive. But she avoided the subject. Even the boys understood that the baby must not be spoken of until she was reborn at the start of the new moon.

Great Mother told Crab and Thistle to stay with Willow at the hillside shelter for a few days. To keep them away from

Mizzle? Willow was beginning to think keeping people out of Mizzle's way accounted for everyone's abrupt departure from the settlement. Would they remain in the valley of trees until the new moon?

Great Mother's stern look was all the warning Willow needed to keep that question to herself. Afterward, she supposed, Great Mother would explain why she had cleared out the settlement. All she would say now was that if Thistle and Crab put their legs to work for the boy, they would not only speed him in his crafting, but they might also learn some useful skills along the way.

Heading out to the hillside, all three were so loaded down with supplies that there was little energy to spare for talk. But when they stopped midway and lowered their packs for a rest, the boys resumed a conversation they must have started earlier.

"If we help with the boat," said Thistle, "the sea might not take it when it takes him."

"It still remains his," Crab replied. "Of his making. With his power."

"What does that matter?" Thistle stretched his aching back. His face was splotched from the bird attack, his hair still encrusted with blood. "We worked for it."

"I am only saying that the uncles may consider it tainted."

"But if it does not go under …"

Willow stood up. She hoisted her pack. "Talk later," she said. "Move now."

Their swift glances informed her of their resentment. As far as the boys were concerned, she was neither Great Mother nor Tall Reed but their childhood companion. She would have to be careful not to overstep her lead. At the same time she needed to guard against their taking the lead themselves.

When they reached the shelter and found no Thorn, Willow was at an immediate advantage. She suggested that they store the bird meat and the skins and bones. They could rest then, unless they wanted to start cooking some bird meat for all of them. Meanwhile, she told them, she would fetch Thorn.

Once again their looks warned that she was treading close to a challenge. Quickly she brushed cold ash from the outdoor fireplace to expose a few live embers. They could start this burning with some of the dry reeds, she suggested, but they must not touch the green ones bound together. She hoped she sounded as though she knew what Thorn planned to do with them. She also hoped the boys wouldn't ask her, since she still had no idea how they were to be used.

Then she strode off to the marsh, where she came upon stacks of cut reeds on the slope above the wetland. Thorn's strange harvest was yielding to his purpose.

This time the dog came splashing to her, his tail spraying her with mud. His greeting spread a rush of gladness through her. It felt like the sun when clouds part and a sudden warmth descends.

"You took a while," said Thorn, still hidden among the reeds. "I have used what rabbit gut I could wrest from the dog. I need stronger bindings."

"Come and eat," she said. "Crab and Thistle are cooking bird meat."

He was clambering up the bank, reeds under one arm, the other hauling and plunging the deer bone so that he could swing his shrunken leg free of the muck. "I am ready for food," he said.

She told him they could all help carry the reeds after their meal. But Thorn still insisted on bringing the newest bundle, so she gathered up another armful from the slope.

On the way to the shelter he veered from the path and beckoned her to join him.

"Those stones," he said, pointing to the ground. "I think they are huts. I used some outer slabs to dig for turf for the fire. When I scooped away the looser soil, I found tools like branches, harder than bone."

"Deer horn," said Willow. "Great Mother says that the Wave covered other hut clusters. She says that when she was a child there were many more people on this land."

"Why does no one look for tools there?" Thorn asked.

"The bones of our people will be there as well. If we leave them undisturbed, they may come back." Like you, she thought, if you are one of the Boundless.

They returned to the path, Willow slowing her steps to walk by his strong side.

As soon as the dog picked up the scent of the cooking bird meat, he forged ahead. But when he caught sight of the boys, he circled around behind Thorn and Willow. After that he maintained a wary distance.

At first the boys backed off in much the same manner as the dog. For his part, Thorn, intent on his boat, barely glanced their way. So with nothing to confront and little to avoid, it didn't take long for them to overcome their uneasiness.

After they had eaten and Thorn's current phase of crafting was under way, first Crab and then Thistle drew close, each unable to resist the lure of the unusual.

"Will there be a tree as well?" Crab asked, as Thorn pulled hard to tighten bound reeds in an overlapping sequence.

"A small tree would be good," said Thorn, squatting and reaching over his useful leg to cover the expanding layer. "Can you get one?" He kept on winding and tightening as he spoke.

"They will soon bring trees to the huts," Crab said.

"A tree would be good."

Crab shot a glance at Thistle, who said, "Great Mother told us to help Willow bring what you asked for and then, maybe, stay to help you, too."

Swiveling and then hopping clumsily, Thorn turned the other way. "A tree would be good," he said once more. Then he stopped and scowled. "Maybe not here. It will be awkward to move a tree with the boat. Later, though, when I am allowed to return to the coast."

"They might not let you," Thistle told him.

"Still," Thorn replied thoughtfully, "I will have to return, one way or another."

"We know," said Thistle.

Nothing more was mentioned about his undetermined fate. But it seemed to Willow that Thorn behaved as though he already knew what was going to happen.

The first thing the boys did was extend Thorn's shelter, the addition only slightly more slipshod than the original. When Thorn first saw it he said to Willow, "Maybe they had better not work on the boat."

Willow laughed. Then she said, "They are better workers than I used to be. If you show them the way you showed me, you may find them useful."

He looked doubtful, but he started them making string.

At first they resisted his method. Their way was simpler and just as effective.

"Then do one your way and one mine," said Thorn, laying out the stems on either side of them. When the boys had used up one clump of stems to make their string, they showed it to Thorn. He poked the bone he had been using into the turf. It was the one with a hole through the blunt end, with string running through it.

While he instructed them in his kind of string-making, Willow touched the smooth surface of the tool. Impulsively she pulled it out of the ground and brushed soil from its fine point. She stared at Thorn's project. With just a glimmer of understanding, she shoved the sharp end beneath a string binding. But it didn't penetrate far enough, so she pulled it out and tried again. This time she aimed the sharpened tip midway through the bound section of reeds. Although it emerged on the other side, it stuck when she tried to pull it all the way through. Grasping it with her thumb and forefinger, she yanked as hard as she could. The bone tool leaped free, but it left the string behind.

She was digging into the tightly bound reeds to extract the lost string when Thorn said mildly, "If you want to use this, you must do it properly."

"I was trying ..." Willow couldn't declare that she had been trying to help him. Thorn would see through her self-righteous defense. Anyway, he seemed to take for granted that she had been meddling. So she said, "I hope I did not spoil anything."

Thorn pulled the string from the direction it had entered the binding. Then with quick, deft fingers he inserted one end of the string through the hole and drew it all the way until there were two equal lengths. Next he showed her how to knot the ends together. When he first drove the bone into and through the binding, he doubled back to tie the knotted ends before continuing.

Fascinated, Willow watched him weave the string through and around, tightening what was already tight. "You keep doing the same thing over and over," she blurted, "even though it is already done."

"This is how my father made the boat I came in. Bones that frame the vessel cannot alone hold it above the waves. Reeds help. By themselves they are frail, but when they are pressed and changed they become strong." While he spoke he kept on pushing and tugging and tightening. "You could do some of this, but only if you understand why you must go through each tiresome step."

Willow nodded. She knew that he was thinking of her customary shortcuts. He must be leery of her undertaking something so vital as this boat.

Crab and Thistle called out that they had finished the second test string. They were pleased with the outcome of their test, because Thorn's method had taken so much longer to complete.

"Bring them," Thorn said.

The boys approached, each with a string.

Thorn asked Willow to fetch a pounding stone and the shoulder blade bone he used for digging. Then, using a scrap of sealskin to protect the flat end, he drove the blunt end into the ground. "Now we are ready," he said, holding out his hand. "First your string."

Grinning, Thistle gave it to him. He seemed to know what Thorn intended.

Thorn flipped one end over the shoulder blade. Then he rolled onto his stomach and held the other end to the ground. "Down," he said. "Ground level. Pull."

Thistle dropped to his knees and grabbed his end. He started to draw back, but Thorn was stronger than he guessed. When yanking failed, he sawed the string from side to side. Then he resumed the jerking. The string was beginning to fray across the shoulder blade. With one great lunge, Thistle rolled, and the string came with him. He yelped in triumph. Then he noticed that he had only part of the string. After an instant's hesitation he demanded Thorn's end so he could measure which was longer.

Thorn showed not the slightest interest in comparative lengths. "Other string," he said, preparing it as he had the first. It was Crab's turn to oppose Thorn. But he pulled in vain. After he had struggled to wrest the string from Thorn's grasp, he let Thistle take his place. Thistle tried every trick he had performed with the first one until Thorn called a halt to the contest.

They all examined this test string, which was slightly abraded where it had been pulled across the blade. Still it was intact. Thorn didn't have to point out that it had been more abused than the first one. He simply told the boys he was glad they had followed his instructions so faithfully. Maybe now he could entrust them with string-making.

"What will you be doing?" Thistle demanded.

"I will finish this section of binding," he said, "and then begin work on the stomachs of the diving birds. There is much to do," he told them cheerfully. "Help is good."

THORN

I could not answer the old woman when she asked who I was. But lately I have begun to believe that I might be connected with the buried settlement. The shadow shapes on the bones tell me so. Yet Willow thinks some of her own people dwelled here. Can I be one with this settlement while a stranger among those on the coast? On the High Island I could not belong to my mother's people, and here I do not belong to my father's.

Maybe this means I am no one.

I cannot tell what Willow thinks of me. She is curious without caring. That is why she pinched my leg. Even when she looks after me, she seems only to hunger for knowledge of what I am. If in the end the sea swallows me, her regret will likely be for my untold story. If she were not so rash, I would try to tell her more of it. But just as I must set aside shadow-making lest it reveal something I do not understand, so must I stay wary of her. Maybe this is just as well, for the boat grows apace.

I am glad of the help she has brought. All the same I find it harder to think through the obstacles that arise. Just when I discover a way to give the boat some feature I recall, I am reminded that appearance is not enough. Father's boat sustained us on a journey I cannot repeat. Yet I will not go cringing from here. My vessel must be worthy of the sea.

I have begun to stitch together the wings, but I still have

to work out how to attach them so that they respond to wind as well as to ropes. If only I did not have to turn aside so often to oversee the boys. Since Thistle resents correction, I rely on Crab to take apart what is wrongly contrived. He is willing to start over, and he is clearly pleased when he accomplishes the appointed task.

Meanwhile Willow, all eagerness, rushes from one blunder to the next. So I keep a close eye on her, too. She can be a tiresome presence, even when she is attentive. If only she did not have to question everything, to know everything.

Sometimes I think she knows more than she realizes. While she listens to the boys, I catch her watching me, to see what I make of them. I suppose she is a kind of weaver, plying thoughts instead of threads. Although I cannot fathom the pattern she weaves, I have a feeling it is unfinished.

WILLOW

The long days with almost unending light were so full, so demanding, that by dusk all essential talk was reduced to a few bare words. Willow kept forgetting to track the moon. It appeared so briefly that if she gave in to exhaustion she missed it.

Dawn always arrived too soon, but Thorn wouldn't allow the others to sleep on. As soon as Willow was roused, she sprang into action. But the boys groaned and grumbled and turned their faces to the dark of the shelter. Only when the embers sputtered to life and hare or duck began to sizzle over a small flame did they stagger to the fireplace to await the morning meal.

Then came a daybreak thick with cloud. The glowering sky hunched over the hillside like a fierce hunting bird poised to strike. The dog crawled into the shelter. Willow and Thorn stoked the fire, but as the first ponderous drops spattered down, they knew it was doomed.

They made a dash for the shelter, where they told each other that this might be a passing downpour. But they knew it was not.

While the boys pulled their cover skins tight around themselves, Thorn and Willow picked up a started rope and in a halfhearted way began to add to it. But they were too close to maintain the necessary tension. Even Thorn had to resign himself to inactivity.

As gusts of wind-driven rain swept across the heath, Thorn murmured something about water collection and storage on the boat. "What kind of skin?" he asked himself.

Willow wondered how much weight the boat could bear. If Thorn was considering skin containers rather than stone, why had he stitched stones into a ridge of bound reeds from one end of the bottom to the other?

She was mulling this, on the verge of asking him, when he said, "After my father's mother and father were brought to the High Island, no one thought they could have come from the Last Island. But your people believe I might be one of the Boundless who live through time. I do not understand why."

Willow thought a moment. Then she asked him, "Do the people of the High Island tell the story of Star the Boundless?"

"We … they have a story about Seed, who reached the Last Island and wanders the sea, boundless."

"Maybe Seed is like Star. He and his companions also wander until they can go no farther. They are at the Last Island."

"Begin again," said Crab sleepily. "Tell the whole of it."

"You know it already. You may listen, but be quiet." Willow turned back to Thorn. "Star and his men spend countless lifetimes in perfect comfort. But then one of them longs for home, for his lost life. Star and his companions are warned not to set foot upon their homeland, for if they do, they will crumble to dust. That is part of the story, Thorn. So when your father would not land his boat upon our beach, my people must have thought of it."

"The men with my father prevented our landing," Thorn told her. "They feared to lose him to his people. In our story

Seed and his men approach an island where people only laugh. As Seed circles the island in search of someone who will speak, one of his companions dives into the water and swims to the island. At once he becomes like the others, caught in everlasting laughter. So he is left there."

Thistle sat up. "I need to move," he said. "The skin above me leaks."

Crab peered overhead. "The gap leaks. You never covered the overlap."

"I never expected this much rain. Besides, I thought we would be away from here by now."

"Think," mused Crab, "not of a few days, but of lifetimes filled with nothing but laughter."

"If there were no leaks and food enough, I would be willing to go to that island," said Thistle.

Willow said to Thorn, "Your story of Seed fits ours somewhat. But Star wanders long upon the pathless sea in search of home. Finally he and his companions head toward a familiar shoreline where folk gather on the beach to greet them."

"Just as we came to your shore? But Father had only heard of your land from his father and mother," said Thorn. "It was familiar only through their telling."

"There is more to the story of Star," Willow told him. "No one recognizes him or his men. When the people on the familiar shore ask who he is and he tells them, all they can say is that Star the Boundless is in their ancient stories."

"So it is somewhat the same for Seed as for Star. In each story the Last Island is where life never ends."

Willow shook her head. "No. For us the Last Island is where all life ends, except for the Boundless. I think," she added. "Sometimes Great Mother tells it one way, sometimes another. But always when Star turns his boat away from the homeland, the man who yearned to return leaps from the vessel and splashes ashore. The instant he stumbles onto the beach he vanishes, and where he stood there is only a small mound of ashes, which the next wave carries off. Then Star's boat glides over the water toward the setting sun and is seen no more."

They sat in the unnatural darkness of the shelter listening to the pounding rain. The dog grunted and tightened into a knot of himself. Even Thistle and Crab fell silent, each a wanderer in the vastness of thought.

When the downpour lightened, they all went outside to let the rain wash them clean. Thorn lurched off, the dog at his heel. Crab and Thistle began to talk about the morning meal they had not eaten. But the fireplace was drenched, not one live ember left.

Willow handed out some dried bird meat, saving a portion for Thorn. But when he returned, his lopsided gait covering ground with surprising speed, he was too excited to pause for food. The rain had filled the marsh, transforming it into a pond. He doubted it would stay that way for long. He needed the boat there to set it afloat. At once!

"Carry it?" exclaimed Thistle in disbelief.

Crab nodded. "The three of us can do it."

Thorn led the way, his ungainly walk exaggerated by the pace he tried to set for them.

Even with the ridge of stones down the center of the bottom, the boat proved light enough for the three of them. They each took hold of a loop, which the boys called handles but which Willow understood to be Thorn's arrangement for managing oars. The rope Willow had used with the tree-boat was fixed at the front of this one. Thorn told her to take the other end before they slid the boat into the swamp pond.

"If it fills with water and sinks," Thistle said, "it will be too heavy to drag out."

"It might not sink at once," Crab remarked. "We should decide how long to leave it in the water."

Willow looked up at the sky. But the pale light was too diffuse behind the rain clouds to show the sun's position, and their shadows barely darkened the saturated heath. She said, "There is no way to measure the time to be allowed."

"Put it in while there is yet enough water," Thorn said, and he began to shove the boat through the resistant reeds.

Willow paid out rope as the boat tipped before settling with a slight bounce. Then it floated quietly until the rope snubbed it short.

For a moment all four of them simply stared.

"There," murmured Thorn, looking gratified.

"It looks like a basket," said Crab.

"Or like a huge nest," Thistle responded. Then he exclaimed, "Think of what we have done!"

Willow had never seen the boys so full of pride. She wondered about Thorn, who was watching the boat with rapt attention, but also with the beginning of a frown.

He said, "We have done nothing unless it will hold at least one of us." When this statement met with utter silence, he started down to the water.

"No," Willow shouted, "not you! It is nothing for one of us to climb out of the mud." She turned to glare at the boys. They returned her look with blank stares, refusing to be caught in this risky venture. So she splashed through the reeds and handed the end of the rope to Thorn, who was already so mired in the flooded marsh that she suspected he would be stuck there until they pulled him free.

Thorn held the boat as still as he could, but as soon as Willow leaned on it to pull herself over the side, it bobbed and dipped. Water poured into it.

"You have to leap in," Crab told her, standing knee-deep in swamp and descending no farther.

"Unless you can fly," Thistle added.

She glanced their way. How quickly they were ready to dismiss what they had achieved. Or were they simply removing themselves from likely failure? She said to Thorn, "Can you bend your leg so I can step on your knee?"

"Yes. Hurry, though. I can scarcely keep my balance here." Holding the boat close, he stabbed the deer bone into the muck and leaned over it to make space for her.

She grabbed his shoulder, then his neck. With both hands clenching fistfuls of his matted hair, she climbed onto his strong leg, at the same moment launching herself and landing face down in the boat.

It dipped again and scooted away from Thorn. Slowly, carefully, she pulled herself into a sitting position. The boat rode lower in the water, but it didn't sink. She looked back at Thorn. The thrust of her plunge must have tipped him sideways, for he was trying to haul himself upright. He raised his head and saw her perched in the center of the boat. He was slathered with mud, but he was beaming.

So were Thistle and Crab. For all Willow knew, they were about to reclaim their part in this wonder. But that didn't seem to matter anymore. What counted was that this strange boat was holding her and it was still afloat.

By the time the boat was pulled into the reed-clogged

mud, she realized that she had no way to step out without swamping it. She said so to Thorn. Then, lest Thistle and Crab distance themselves once more, she declared that beaching it on sand would be a simpler matter.

After that she made a mess of it, for the water wasn't deep enough to tread and the bottom wasn't firm enough to support her. All she could do was cling to the side of the boat, dragging it down until it filled with slime.

In the end both Thistle and Crab had to help Thorn pull her and the boat out. All four of them struggled against the drag of mire that sucked them down. By the time they were on solid ground, with the boat upended to drain, they were content to stretch out their mud-caked limbs and rest.

Thorn, the first to comment, sounded a note of caution. "It needs the other bird stomachs," he murmured. "Yes, and higher sides." He sat up.

"How much higher?" asked Willow, thinking of clambering in and out of the craft.

Thorn placed one flat palm above the other. "Two hands, maybe three."

Thistle groaned. "I thought it was finished," he said.

"It might not matter anyway. It may already be the time of the new moon," said Crab.

"We can carry reeds back with us on the boat," Thorn told them. "That way no time will be lost."

Willow thought the boys might refuse to reenter the swamp. But the boat lying upside down before them possessed its own pulling power now that it was so close to completion. It had known their touch; they were a part of its making.

Hungry and exhausted though they were, they followed

Thorn and Willow back into the muck to harvest the necessary reeds.

Late in the day they staggered back to the shelter bearing the boat laden with reeds.

Thorn, scarcely able to propel himself forward, lagged behind with the dog.

So he was the last to discover that a band of people from the settlement had crested the rise and was descending the hill. Willow sensed something momentous. These were not women and children, but her father and Uncle Redstone and other men.

By the time she and the boys had lowered the boat to the ground, the men were striding to meet them.

Willow's father said, "With all that rain, I would have expected to find you clean."

The three regarded one another. They had given no thought to the sticky mud from their labors in the marsh. The morning's washing belonged to the past. In their new present they were more than bedraggled; they were changed.

"What have you done with the boy?" asked Uncle Redstone. His gaze shifted over their heads. He must have caught sight of Thorn.

"What have you done to him?" Willow's father demanded, his tone implying that if they had wronged Thorn, they had dishonored him.

The three simply waited for Thorn to draw near.

"He speaks for himself," muttered Thistle.

"What?" the men asked.

Willow said, "He made a new kind of boat. It is nearly done. We tried it out, and it is not quite finished." She didn't know how to continue. She wanted to plead for more time. They were so close now. If only they could have another day or so.

Uncle Redstone said, "He will have no need of a boat."

"But Great Mother told us to help …"

"Great Mother grows foolish." Willow's father spoke gently as if to inform her of a sickness or death that he supposed would sadden her. "We are released from her command. In the valley of the trees she tried to speak to us of shadow shapes. She would have given false counsel had we permitted it. What knowledge she possessed is tainted now. She is to be disregarded."

Willow wanted to protest. She said, "Not many days ago she pronounced—"

"Willow, have you not noticed the signs of frailty? Small signs, like mislaying tools and repeating sayings and speaking senselessly. These could be borne until her guidance went awry. If wisdom abandons her, so must we."

Willow felt a chill creep through her. Making an effort to keep her voice level and deliberate, she said, "All the knowing of the people is in her."

"It is seeping out," Uncle Redstone said. "Like a container with a spreading crack."

"Something happened," said Crab. "We have not been away very long. Everyone went for the trees. Great Mother turned us back. She told us—"

"Much happened," Uncle Redstone said to him. "She should not have kept you from the trees, and she should not have sent you here to help make … that. It will not be needed."

Thorn dragged himself toward them, but stopped short. He said quietly, "It is needed. The boat. To carry me away."

"The signs are clear now," Willow's father told him. "You will speak and be heard. You will tell us how to save the People of the Singing Seals, and we will do your bidding."

"What signs?" asked Thistle. "He is still maimed."

"We will care for him," said Uncle Redstone. "He will grow strong and heal. We will grow strong and heal. The girl child thrives. Minnow."

"Minnow?" asked Willow.

"Minnow. Her name. This boy comes from the Last Island, where the Boundless dwell. The Wave took our people. This boy is going to bring them back with one fine birth after another. The Wave nearly finished our story. This small Minnow begins it anew."

Willow looked skyward. Was there a new moon? Did she dare ask? All she could see were vast reaches of gray. It could have been the sea suspended above her. Had the world turned upside down?

Her father understood. He said, "Two nights ago. The new moon."

She nodded. She wanted to ask about Great Mother, but she was afraid of what they would tell her. Had they driven her into the sea, as they had planned to do with Thorn?

The men ignored Thorn's protests. If he must have the boat, then the boys and Willow could bring it along. But he should not spend another night in banishment. From now on he would live in their midst, where there would always be someone close by to carry out his bidding.

Uncle Redstone lifted him up and bore him away. Willow's father and the other men followed right behind, as close as possible.

Willow and Crab and Thistle hoisted up the boat. It was considerably heavier now that it had been soaked and contained reeds. Thistle wanted to empty them out, but Crab and Willow wouldn't let him. Willow said slyly, "You heard the uncles. We are to do Thorn's bidding."

For a while they tried to keep up, but their part of the homeward procession straggled and faltered. Finally, on the crest of the hill, they decided to drag the boat down the slope.

The others were far ahead now. The sight of Thorn, draped across Uncle Redstone's shoulders, reminded Willow of the occasional deer the men brought home from the trees. Was he frightened? She didn't think so. As far as she could tell, nothing seemed to make him afraid. Maybe he didn't yet grasp that he had become trophy instead of prey. Or was he simply dazed, too bewildered to fathom this swift reversal? She gazed after him as he was borne away.

Then she looked back at the shelter. The dog was there, nosing around, restless but prepared to wait for Thorn's return. She was tempted to run back, to coax him to come with her. She doubted he would, though. Maybe she could try to fetch him in the morning.

When the dragging began and they could feel the bottom of the boat snag on woody stems, she told the boys to wait while she ran back to the shelter for hauling skins. They promptly sat down, glad for the rest, while she took off.

The dog stood, without approaching, his tail awag, his eyes expectant. Willow pointed in the direction the procession had taken. She said to him, "They took him. You come. I will bring you to him."

The dog dropped to his haunches, the scarred, one-eared head erect, and went still. So she scrambled in and out of the shelter, grabbing any tools she thought Thorn might want, and rolled them hastily inside skins. She turned to go, realized she needed string and rope, and snatched up all she could see.

Before leaving, she paused and walked over to the dog. For the first time she placed her hand on his shoulder, then on the side of his head. He looked out of yellow eyes that gleamed, a steady gaze that met and held her own. It was wrenching to turn away.

Despite the load in her arms, she started at a run and kept it up until the steep incline forced her to slow. By the time she reached the boys, she was gasping. She flung down the skins. The tools tumbled onto the ground. Thistle lunged for one, but Crab blocked him.

"Thorn's," said Crab. "His." He and Willow picked up the scattered tools and deposited them in the boat.

"We can bring other things later," Willow said.

The boys nodded. It was late, and they were tired and hungry.

Crab said, "There might be a feast."

With food thoughts to lift their spirits, they pressed on. But it was true dark by the time they staggered into the settlement, and there was no sign of any cooking fire.

Hungry though she was, Willow really wanted nothing more than sleep. The boys had already disappeared inside the passage when she decided to collect the tools and stow them out of sight. Where? A shallow hole would do for now. She rummaged under the reeds, feeling for each tool, then used the broken deer horn to dig.

Crouched over the littered ground, she probed and then clawed out sandy soil until all at once she became aware of another presence. Two yellow spots shone as the one-eared dog thrust his muzzle at her knees. As soon as she sat back on her heels, he commenced to dig where she had begun. She heard sand and broken shells spray around and behind him. She heard his light panting. She heard from down inside the huts the thin wail of an infant.

"Good," she whispered to the dog as she dropped all the tools into the hole. Leaning forward, she used her arms to shovel the loosened debris on top. Good enough for now, she thought. Still, she took another moment to spread shells from the heap over the spot, so that in the morning light no depression would be visible there. Rising, she told him, "Now you can go to Thorn."

The dog walked beside her down to the entryway, then hesitated.

"Come," she whispered.

She went ahead, then stopped at the opening to the work place. So did the dog. She reached down to his shoulder, along his back where his coat usually lay smooth. The hair stood up from his body. He backed away from under her hand, turned, and retreated.

Puzzled, she remained in the opening. She tried to think how Thorn would deal with the dog. He would go after him, she decided. Then let him, she thought. Let Thorn call the dog to him.

She stepped into the work place, probing with her bare feet, treading with care to avoid bumping into anything that would make a noise. She had to feel for the halfwall in the corner. There. The missing slab had been replaced. That must mean that the shadow creatures had escaped notice. She would deal with them in the morning. Right now all she could do was wake Thorn and let him know that the dog had shied away from the doorway, probably put off by the scent of the others, especially Uncle Redstone, who had carried Thorn here.

Feeling her way slowly, she squeezed through the gap. Then she crouched low. She didn't want to startle Thorn. His sleeping breaths were rougher than usual, almost labored. Well, it had been a long, hard day, full of challenge, of upheaval.

"Thorn," she murmured. "Thorn, wake up."

A harsh breath broke into a small gasp.

"Thorn, the dog is confused. He—"

"Shh!" came a response, followed by stirrings. "Willow, why are you here?" The speaker wasn't Thorn.

Willow drew back in alarm. "Where is he?"

"Shh," Great Mother said to her. "Sit. Be still, child. The boy has been taken into a hut. No doubt he is sleeping, as you should be. We will speak later."

"Why are you in Thorn's place?" Willow asked. "The dog knew."

"The dog probably knows a deal more than most of our people just now," said Great Mother wryly. "I am here because then no one else will be. So far I have been able to keep others from seeing what Thorn has made here. I suppose you know what I speak of?"

Willow said, "I meant to tell you. So much happened."

"We will deal with this as we are able, but not now. You must leave. And Willow, do not let anyone see us together like this."

"But why?" Willow forgot to keep her voice low.

"Hush!" Great Mother said. "Because the people have

turned against me, against their Keeper of Story. They have pulled loose from their past to drift rootless on every fitful wind. This means that when they discover the shadow beasts, their regard for Thorn will likely change. He is safe for a while, you less so. No more now. Leave."

Willow stubbed a toe on something as she groped her way out. The sudden pain brought tears to her eyes. Instead of going to her hut and her bed closet, she turned outside. Already the sky was growing pale, the moon a sliver of light low on the horizon.

She had no trouble returning to the boat. Creeping into it, she helped herself to one of the dragging skins, lifted the damp reeds, and stacked them to make a space for herself. The damp went through her. Given time, she thought, some warmth would come. But she lay there clenched with worry and cold.

The dog came. He stood tall, as though surveying the area. Then he jumped into the boat and settled with a grunt by her side. Almost at once warmth flowed from him to her. She slept.

THORN

Is this then what my father expected when he brought me here? For me to be given a favored sleeping place and the first portion of bird meat from the fire? It feels strange, this welcome.

While I am honored so, I am still mindful of the fear that gripped me when I thought they would feed me to the sea. To quell that fear I told myself that I would join my sister, although I wondered how we would recognize each other. I supposed it would be easier for me than for someone with two legs who might swim for a while and try to stay afloat. I knew from before, from when I fell from the tipping boat, that I would go under quickly.

That was what led me to the idea of a boat that would not tip over, a boat of my own crafting. At first it was a way to stave off the helplessness ahead. But that is changing. As the boat takes shape, it seems to gain a life of its own, so that at times I almost forget that its fate is linked with mine. And I sense more power in it than I have known. While I am eager to see it finished, I do not want its making to end.

Have I lost my way? As I am watched, my mother grows more distant. It seems that I must be alone for her to come. If I were alone now, I would make her shadow shape to keep her in my sight. If I were alone, I would listen for my father's voice, and he would tell me if my choice is right.

But I am not alone. Day and night these people stay near.

They say they keep me safe. I offer no reply. I accept their favor. Never before have I pretended one thing while thinking and planning another. I wish I knew what Father would say. Would he approve, or would he condemn such deception?

Willow has already started to bind the reeds. She uses my fire stone now so that she can split more roots to make string. She has the boys helping her, but she does not let the fire stone out of her hands. She promises to return it to me when this task is finished.

I would like her to keep it. I wish I could tell her that I will have no need of it in the sea. But I do not think she will assist in my escape if she discerns my true intent.

So I continue unresisting and calm.

When I asked for the spreading link of the whale back-bone, I was not certain it could become a strong enough base within the boat. But it seems to fit. It must be fastened firmly at the front and on each side, so that when the stripped tree is lodged in the hollow core of the backbone, it will bear the pressure of wind on wing.

I am less certain of the wing I have fashioned from true wings stitched together. If only I could take the boat to sea, using first one method and then another, I might learn what I need to guide the boat. But this will not be allowed. When Thistle offered to try out the boat in my place, Willow frowned and shook her head to warn me against him.

I tell myself it does not matter whether the wing takes the wind and the boat surmounts the waves, for neither wing nor boat has to prevail for very long. But I cannot abandon what I have crafted. In truth I long for it to bear me away with measured force, and yet with the look of wild flight. I want to feel it soar.

This may be what makes Willow and the boys share my resolve, for they do not seem to doubt my destination across the sea. So they work as never before, and no one mentions how or when I will go, only that the time for my departure draws near.

But I feel a river of sadness, or maybe regret, flowing beneath Willow's steadfast efforts. She, too, grows crafty. Only once has she mentioned Great Mother, and that was to pass along the old woman's warning that the people's trust may shift and shift again. Great Mother believes it will take little, just a setback or two, for them to conclude that I bring them misfortune. I suppose she is right, for they examine me daily for signs of improvement in my shrunken leg. In time they are bound to notice that it does not change.

But I will not await this turn of events. It would be too mean, too accidental. I will go as I must.

Still, with little time left, I have begun to wonder why my departure must end everything we have made. After all, I leave behind the idea of my boat. Willow and Crab and Thistle could craft another, which might be tried and found flawed and then improved until it works. And that one might be followed by still another, until one is made sound enough to carry them to some undiscovered shore. Is such hope foolish?

Already Crab has begun to arrange new workings on his own. When he proposed to fashion sealskin storage containers along the inner sides of the boat for food and water and tools and covers, at first I started to put these off. But I realized in time that I must appear to expect that my journey will be long. Quickly I said that such preparations might alert my watchers to my escape. I also explained that I could catch fish in my net. Crab replied that he and Thistle had let it be known that they themselves expected to use the boat to bring home all manner of creatures from the sea.

Now I guard my tongue. Crab and Thistle are so intent on the craft that they do not question how I will handle the steering oar and the wing. But then I catch a glimpse of Willow staring at me with narrowed eyes. When she sees that I have noticed, she looks away.

This is what happened when I told Crab that containers were not needed. It made me uneasy. Willow sees where others do not. I try to take even greater care with her. I show her how to apply the fire stone to the oar that will serve for either paddling or steering. None of these efforts will be wasted, I tell her, for they teach all of us ways that have not been tried before, at least by our people.

Her people. As for those I came from, even if I could hold the boat on course, I still would not know how to return to the High Island. Nor would my mother's people take me back. They gave my baby sister to the sea and they refused to keep me.

How strange, then, to flee the People of the Singing Seals now that they have ceased their dislike of me.

But just now they like me too well. Or they like the idea of me.

WILLOW

Willow had no trouble finding Great Mother alone. She simply took advantage of everyone's fascination with Thorn. Renewed fascination, no longer driven by revulsion. Now when people stared at his leg, it was to discern the earliest evidence of regrowth.

Their unrelenting attention to Thorn was frightening.

In the dimness of the walled corner of the work place she asked Great Mother whether something else drastic had happened when she tried to speak to the people about shadow shapes.

"It was nothing drastic, Willow. I hoped to lead their thoughts in new directions." Great Mother shook her head. "They would not budge. They were unyielding."

Willow scowled. How could that account for such a transformation? "But all at once? They veered so far, so fast."

Great Mother said, "It is not as sudden as you think. You have been absent awhile. Not away, but absent even when you were here with us. You have spent much time alone or with Thorn, so you did not see what was coming."

"What about Thistle and Crab?" asked Willow, for the boys had seemed bewildered by the change, too.

"The boys may be troubled. That is because they do not look beneath the look of things. It would be well for you to keep them attached to the boat. Thorn has even greater need of them now than before, when I first sent them to the hillside."

Willow didn't think it would be hard to keep them attached to the boat. But when she recalled Thistle throwing stones and relishing the prospect of driving Thorn into the sea, she wondered what his help might cost. She could see that he hungered for all the understanding and skills Thorn could provide. She said, "I am not certain Thorn can rely on Thistle."

Great Mother thought a moment. Then she said, "You are right. Thistle is like a dog that pounces on the weakest vole. Now that I am out of favor with the people, I may seem to him like that vole, an irresistible prey. So do not mention me when you speak of Thorn's escape. Depend on Crab. Let Crab decide when and how to rally Thistle and to keep him from betraying Thorn."

Willow said, "How can I leave you out?"

"Only with the boys, Willow. It matters little whether they disregard or even despise me. Think only of Thorn. Go now. The boat must be readied. It must be close to the beach and remain that way for several days until the watchers are accustomed to seeing it there."

"But they will continue to watch, especially when Thorn is with it. And at night they make certain he is in his bed closet."

"I have thought of that. Soon there must be a feast, which means there must first be a great hunt. Seal, I think. I have seen the seals follow Thorn and call to him. I have heard him answer in a voice like theirs. He sings them to the shallows."

"Thorn believes that if you listen well to beasts, you will know how to speak with them."

"That may be true," Great Mother replied. "But I think the listener in him is part of his being a maker."

Listener, yes. But a speaker of truth? Not for the first time

Willow found herself wondering about this. She longed for Great Mother's understanding. But what could she say? That now and again something in Thorn's manner or word made her skin tighten as if danger lurked? How could she explain the instant chill that forced her to draw back, to watch him and try not to show that she was doing so? "Sometimes ..." She faltered.

"Go, Willow. Begin to prepare for the feast to come."

"The feast? Oh, yes. But why?" Willow asked.

"The people will gorge themselves as always. Only Thorn and you and the boys will eat lightly. One of you must take Thorn's place, wrapped in a skin cover. The other two will send him off upon the water."

"You speak as you always do. Are you not ... sad?"

Great Mother smiled. "Time for sadness after we have saved that boy. Then we may be sad because of what we have lost in him."

"But I mean sad for yourself," Willow blurted.

Great Mother shook her head. "No, I am weary. My life is almost finished. If I leave behind a Keeper of Story like you, it has not been in vain."

"I could never be what you have been," Willow mumbled. "I do not understand my own people. I do not understand why they turn on you and expect the impossible from Thorn."

Great Mother said, "When despair goes deep, people grasp at any hopeful sign within their reach. Faith in Thorn could bring renewed vigor and purpose to our people. It could even sweep them past the earliest setbacks that are bound to come, be they famine or sickness or loss. But after a while the people will decide to assign blame. They will not have to cast their net very wide, for unless Thorn makes his escape, he who appeared to bring hope will be as close as an arm length, as good as caught."

Like the vole, thought Willow. The vole that is ready prey.

As soon as Willow found her father alone, she appealed to him. "You and Uncle Redstone and the others have changed so much. Great Mother has changed only in small ways. Can you not see that?"

Her father said, "We relied on her for too long. Misfortune followed misfortune."

"Not of her doing," Willow insisted.

Willow's father placed his hands on her shoulders and brought his face close to hers. "It is a sorry thing to charge an old woman with false telling. But she disregards our needs and bestows upon us a scattering of senseless notions. If we allowed even one such notion, she would cast doubt on another belief and then another until all we hold true would be lost to us."

Willow gave up trying to defend Great Mother. It helped that she had so much to do, so much to learn while Thorn remained with them.

Later, much later, it came to Willow that neither she nor Great Mother had dealt with the shadow creatures on the inside face of the slabs. How long would they be safe from probing eyes? Why had Great Mother neglected to mention them again? Was this yet another instance of her forgetfulness?

Yet in the urgent press of each passing day, Willow, too, had let the shadow creatures slip from her thoughts.

Willow sought out Crab and then had to wait until he was by himself. She had intended to speak about Thorn's escape, but as soon as they were alone together, words fled and she was left floundering. What, after all, did Crab understand? Maybe he really did believe that the boat was being readied for fishing.

"What do you suppose will happen to the boat?" she finally asked.

The question surprised him. "Happen?" He looked at her inquiringly. "You mean happen to Thorn?" He spoke bluntly, almost impatiently. "It is hard to say. He is closely watched. They will not risk losing him. But—" Crab broke off, scowling. When he spoke again, his voice was low, and he chose his next words cautiously. "Thorn would not treat the boat with such care if he did not plan a long journey."

Still feeling her way, Willow said, "Then he will need our help."

Crab nodded. "Even so, he is unlikely to escape. He is never alone."

When Willow told Crab what needed to be done, he pulled back, refusing to bring Thistle into any secret plan. "Thistle is too quick to boast. He shares his exploits with anyone willing to hear about them."

"But these plans are not yet deeds," Willow protested. Only when she remembered how Thistle had blurted out his account of the rescue on the stack did she back down and agree to keep most of their plan from him until they could be more certain of his loyalty. For now, he could help carry the boat to the beach. Afterward, with the prospect of launching it at hand, maybe they would be able to reach an understanding with him.

"But it cannot be done all at once," Crab said to Willow. "Not without telling too much, risking too much."

Willow nodded, grateful for Crab's concern. Meanwhile

she found it harder to talk with Thorn. Even when they were at work on the boat, their heads bent to a task and close together, only a few words could pass between them.

Willow waited for an opportunity. The chance finally came when Crab called Thistle away, leaving Willow and Thorn together attaching the whalebone to the boat.

"This is weaving," Thorn told Willow. "Over and under. It is how to connect fibers that run across each other."

"Fibers do not run," Willow said loudly. Then she lowered her voice. "But you will. As soon as the boat is ready, you must call the seals. Call them for a kill."

"I do not kill what I call," Thorn told her softly. "Pull tighter."

"It cannot get any tighter," she retorted in her big voice. Then, quiet again, she said, "You have to. For a feast. Afterward everyone will sleep soundly. That is how you get away." She heard Crab and Thistle arguing about the merits of seal bone and sheep bone. "Crab is with us," she added hurriedly. "He is trying to find out whether Thistle ..." At Crab's approach she fell silent.

Crab deposited bones that Thorn had requested. "Sheep bones splinter too easily," Crab declared, and then he lowered his voice to say, "Thistle will help."

Willow nodded. Thorn nodded. "Now consider the use of light bone against the use of bone that is stronger but heavier." Thorn's voice was intended to be heard. "Which is needed more, lightness or strength?"

The uncle who was watching over Thorn yawned and scratched his head. He wasn't interested in the relative merits of the bones.

"These sides bend if you lean against them. The bones are

to keep them rigid against the slosh of waves," said Thorn.

"If only we could try each kind of bone," said Thistle.

"Time," said Willow.

Crab hefted first one bone, then another.

Thorn's tone became light, his manner almost carefree. He said softly, "If I leave behind my things … tools … some of them, how will you put them to use?"

Thistle looked up from the bones, sharp-eyed, making no attempt to mask his greed. Willow felt a chill of alarm. Had Crab misjudged Thistle? Was this eagerness for a contest between them, or simply for the things themselves? Maybe neither. Thistle might be tempted above all by the trembling vole at his mercy. Willow could see how alert he was as he summoned his best response.

"I would build another boat. More boats," he declared.

Thorn directed an inquiring glance at Crab, who said at once, "I would make more tools."

Thorn smiled. Then, without looking at her, he said, "And how would Willow use the fire stone, if I could leave it behind?"

She flushed. He was testing her, but not in the way he had tested the boys. Was he trying to determine her grasp of his true intention?

Wondering how to avoid his trap, she decided to set one for him. "You will need the fire stone to make repairs, and to hunt at sea," she told him. "Unless your landfall is nearby."

Leaning forward, his palms on the edge of the boat, Thorn seemed to look past Willow, seaward. "Coming here, we glimpsed many possible landing places before we found the stack my father sought. But each time we drew close to shore, we could see no smoke, no shell or bone heap, nor any other sign of life, only the scoured faces of hut walls half buried in sand." He straightened, as if suddenly recalling Willow's probing remark. "Anyhow," he told her, "near or far matters little if there is food in the containers."

"Still," Willow retorted, "you will need to hunt to feed the dog as well as yourself."

"No!"

Thorn's muted cry caught the attention of the uncle whose watch it was. He started to his feet. Then, having seen nothing amiss, he settled back down, tipped his face to the sun, and half closed his eyes.

"No dog," Thorn said, trying to regain control of his voice, his feelings.

Thistle came to Thorn's rescue, pointing out that the dog would upset the boat's balance and get in Thorn's way.

Willow nodded as if persuaded. Then she led the talk back to bones.

How she ached to race off, straight to Great Mother. She had to force herself to wait, though, so that her departure would seem natural, unconnected to Thorn's outcry. She allowed herself a brief glance in his direction. Once again his look was bland, his eyes, like his voice, revealing nothing more than his usual preoccupation with the boat's finishing touches.

"Great Mother!" Willow caught sight of her on the path to the hill. "Great Mother, wait!" But the bent figure moved steadily on.

Willow pelted after her.

Just as Willow caught up with her, the old woman whipped around. "Not here. Not now." She turned back to the path.

Willow, breathless, couldn't stop. "I found out who he

is," she gasped. She plunged on. "Thorn. I know, because he means to give himself to the sea. Thorn!" The words burst from her. "He is one of the Boundless. He must be. He can be no other. Great Mother, hear me!"

Great Mother spoke facing straight ahead. "I hear you. Let us hope no one else does." Her pace quickened.

Willow glanced around. "There is no one near."

"Still," said Great Mother, "we can be seen."

"But we often are together," Willow exclaimed. "It is expected."

"Not anymore," Great Mother told her. "Now it can only lead to disfavor."

"Why not favor? You and I are the first to know this truth. When you tell the people, their regard for you will be restored."

"Willow, that is what they already believe. Have you not understood that it is why your father and uncle and the others are determined to keep Thorn from slipping away?"

This brought Willow up short. She struggled to rearrange her argument. "But they only believe," she said. "You have often said that belief is part hope. Now they will *know*."

Great Mother let a small sigh escape her lips. She looked frail and small enough to be flattened by the breeze that scoured the grasses all around her. "What do you think they will know?" she asked wearily.

"All the preparation. The making of this winged boat. I thought ..." Willow faltered. "I thought it meant Thorn had chosen his destination. Whether the High Island or some landfall along this coast where stone dwellings were sighted, it was a place he meant to reach."

Great Mother swayed a little, then spread her feet to brace

against a gust of wind. "Then?" she prompted. "Then something changed?"

Willow nodded. All at once she felt less sure. This often happened with Great Mother. "I found out," she repeated, struggling to regain the excitement that had surged through her. "I tricked him." She had to force a note of triumph. "There is no destination. He means only to leave us. He may wander like Star until the sea takes him. So ..." She faltered. What else could she say? Why did Great Mother's expression remain so severe? Where was her amazement?

Great Mother set off again along the narrow path. After a moment she said, "I have always thought he meant to go that way. How did you learn of his intent?"

"The dog." Willow, following Great Mother, told her about Thorn's reaction. "He might have been a bit worried that I suspected something. So while he set about to trap me into revealing what I thought, I trapped him with talk of the dog." Great Mother's chuckle gave Willow heart. "I knew he would never take the dog into the sea."

"Clever Willow. A worthy match in trickery. But his is a different kind of craftiness. He is a true maker. And not only of nets and boats."

Willow guessed Great Mother was speaking again of the shadow creatures in Thorn's corner. Shunned, she had protected them by staying there. So why had she left now? "Where are you going?" Willow asked from behind her.

Great Mother stopped. "Where am I going? What you tell me has scattered my thoughts. If I go on, I expect I may recall the purpose of my journey."

"But," Willow blurted, "if you already knew Thorn to be Boundless, how can my discovery scatter your thoughts?"

Great Mother faced her again. "Not Boundless," she said. "Not where he would go, Willow, only how. All you tricked him into revealing was his determination to meet his fate on his own."

"Because he cannot die!" Willow exclaimed. "Because he knows he is Boundless."

Shaking her head, Great Mother said softly, "No. Because he knows too well what it is like to be helpless."

Willow gazed at the wrinkled face and into the pale eyes that had once been the color of the sea in sunlight. "You would let him go like that?" she asked. It came to her that Great Mother had arranged for Thorn to make the boat. "Did you want him to? Did you know what would happen?"

Great Mother shook her head again. "I did not," she said. "At the outset I knew nothing. Then I heard the boy decide. That was when I understood that I might help him carry out his plan. The rest was up to him."

Willow was silenced. It was hard to absorb all that Great Mother accepted. How could Willow agree with her? How could she have been so wrong about Thorn? "You are certain he is not one of the Boundless?" Willow asked.

Great Mother nodded. She walked on.

Willow stood rooted on the path. What if she opposed Thorn's decision? Could she persuade him against an intention he refused to acknowledge? If she spoke of it, he would sidestep the matter, leaving her confused and foolish. She knew him well enough to realize that he would go his own way whatever she said, unless … She glanced at the bent figure walking away from her. Great Mother had declared Willow a worthy match. Well, then, was there a way to trick Thorn one more time?

Willow took a deep breath and dashed after Great Mother.

When she drew abreast of her, she said, "Do come back now. We need you. We are not finished. Besides, there will be a hunt, a feast. Remember?"

"Of course I remember," Great Mother snapped. "I am not so feeble and forgetful as I sometimes seem."

Willow felt the heat rush into her face. "I know, I know," she stammered. "But if you do not remember where you were heading, why not return to where you are needed? There is much to do."

"Or nothing," Great Mother said. "Nothing to do but see to the hunt and the feast."

Willow almost blurted out what was taking shape in her thoughts. Instead she simply pleaded. "So much can go awry. Who else can I speak to if you are gone?"

Great Mother said, "Help me down. I will rest awhile. I must consider ..." As her words trailed off, her scrawny arm reached toward Willow for support, and she sank slowly to the ground.

THORN

Something has happened. Has been happening through these days of work and crafting. Now purpose and tasks bind us, and we are separate no longer. That is why I stumbled when Willow spoke of the dog. Did she mean to trip me up? Even though she joins in my effort, sometimes she seems to oppose me. It is strange to grow close and yet to stand at a distance. We are like two wary dogs that circle each other.

So concealment is still needed.

To quell any doubt that may have crept into Willow's thinking, to show that I am preparing for landfall, I let Willow and Crab and Thistle know why I took apart the wing ropes to arrange them anew. I explained that my father had shown me how a wing that could swing would hold a boat against shifting winds and allow it to pass through rocky shallows to land. Even though I know how unlikely it is that I could beach the boat unaided, at least some good may come from this deception, for in time, when the others make their own boats, the wings should not only carry them to sea but bring them safely to shore.

When I nearly gave away my true purpose, the one I cannot share with any other person, I discovered the danger that dwells within closeness, within trust. With every task that was linked to another, so were we linked, each of us intent on the whole.

I could not keep from wondering how it would feel to hold

nothing back. In my wonder I devised another outcome. It included Willow and the boys and the dog, all of us setting forth to seek a beginning place. It beguiled me, that wonder, holding me captive. There we would dig together, clearing out one buried hut and then another, filling them with fire and voices, making a place of our own. Thinking of that life together, I nearly lost my resolve.

So I remind myself that Willow will soon take Great Mother's place, that Crab and Thistle will become leaders of the People of the Singing Seals, and that alone, even with the dog, I could not survive without others.

As the time for my leaving draws near, maybe this is all I need to know.

WILLOW

While Great Mother dozed beside the path, Willow hovered impatiently. She couldn't remain still. Thorn tore at her thoughts, forcing her to pace and circle as she sorted through what was possible and what was not. If only Great Mother would listen to her idea. Well, she would have to before long.

Willow's pacing took her farther off. When she then glanced back to where Great Mother reclined, the terrible thought struck her that the old woman might be dying. Not yet! Willow nearly cried aloud. Not now! She charged across the slope to check. Anxiously Willow stooped down, peering at the face that was turned aside and streaked with wisps of hair.

"I am still alive," Great Mother growled without opening her eyes.

Unnerved, Willow drew back.

Great Mother groaned and propped herself up. "So," she said, "you have the shape of an idea, and you want my approval."

"Yes. No. I want you to tell me what is wrong with it. Whether it can be carried out."

Great Mother plucked a handful of grass and rubbed it all over her face. "Speak, then," she said. "I am ready to listen."

Willow dropped to her knees so that their eyes would meet on the same level. She said, "I will go with Thorn."

Great Mother squinted at her. "Into the sea?"

"No, Great Mother. To keep him from it. He will head for land for my sake."

Great Mother nodded. She seemed to be waiting for Willow to show more of this plan's shape.

So Willow plunged on. "I know he would not willingly take me. But I can hide. It will be in the dark of night. It will be rushed. I can do it."

"Yes," Great Mother responded. "I think you can. But you have not considered the after time. It is not only the risk you would face that troubles me. It is what you would leave behind. Willow, your father and the others are not entirely mistaken about me. You and I know that I have not lost all my wits, but it is true that I am losing my grip on many things. So you cannot carry out the plan you speak of."

"Why not? What about the after time for Thorn? That matters, too."

"It does," Great Mother agreed. "But in spite of what you think of our people and their dismissal of me, you possess more of our story than any other person. They will have need of it."

"Are you telling me to let Thorn go?"

Great Mother shook her head. "Your plan did not surprise me, Willow, because I had already considered it for myself. We are more alike than you realize."

Perplexed, Willow mulled this over. Great Mother concealed on the boat? Thorn and a forgetful old woman alone together on the pathless sea?

"You cannot," she blurted. "You would be lost. Both of you."

"And you would not?"

"I think of heading straight out until we are gone from

sight. After that we might turn partly landward if the wind allows. Then we follow the coastline so that we may find ... arrive somewhere. We can look for an old dwelling from the time before the Wave. And we will have rowing oars as well as the steering one."

Great Mother nodded. "Well thought, well spoken. But Willow, you are needed here. The worst that can happen to Thorn is what he now intends, and the worst that can happen to me is already under way. I will go with Thorn. If we should land where life is possible, who knows what else may be in store for him? Besides," she added, "you underestimate him if you think he would go off in the boat in your absence. He expects you to assist in his departure. What would he think if you failed to appear? He would suspect some trickery. He would not go."

Willow let all of this sink in. She began to realize that by confiding in Great Mother she had trapped herself. But what else could she have done? Was she to lose both Great Mother and Thorn at the same time?

Once again, she thought bitterly, she was to be left out, left behind. Then the rush of resentment that usually crammed her every thought just drained away, leaving nothing but emptiness in its place. She recalled the time before Thorn when a floating tree or a beached whale stood out like a peak on a flat horizon, and she knew she was staring at the sameness of her days to come. There was truth in this sight. There was bleakness.

She let her thoughts unravel. After a while she began to regather them, to form a different pattern, another outlook. First Great Mother, whose quest for their people's fragmented story was already a part of Willow. Next Thorn. Willow couldn't fathom why he always seemed to nettle her, at least until she was able to make sense of his ways. But she did know that some of those ways were now her own. If his leaving stripped her world of meaning, she must find what she could of it within herself. Hadn't she, too, become a maker? And not only of rope and fish traps and almost wings. That making wasn't finished. She and the boys should craft another boat, one to carry them forth in search of Thorn. In search of Great Mother, too, if she lived long enough. Could they? All that work without Thorn's driving vision? If so, what would such a journey entail without a known destination? What did it feel like to go beyond sight of land? Seeking.

It came to her that Great Mother knew all about seeking. She had been away when Thorn first arrived. She had told Willow then, as before, that she had been seeking, but she never said what it was she sought.

"Great Mother," Willow asked her, "what do you look for when you go away?"

"It depends on the time, on the season."

"When Thorn came," prompted Willow.

"Oh, let me see. I think … I think I was searching for … home."

"But your home is—" Willow checked herself. Great Mother was speaking of her childhood home before the Wave altered the land. Willow tried to see Great Mother as a child then, after seawater and ashes from the sky filled every dip and hollow, leaving behind a swath of gray death. How long did it take before birds returned with seeds and the heath grasses slowly took root? By then nothing of Great Mother's lost home remained above ground.

Willow held out her hand. "Soon you will have no need of it," she said, "because you will be on the boat."

Great Mother took the proffered hand in both of hers. "Until my last breath," she said, "that need will be in me." She paused. "But do not grieve for me, Willow. I am not bereft. The time has come to think of Thorn, who has yet to know a true home."

Willow was so intent on the timing of their plan that she didn't worry about failure until Thistle remarked to Tall Reed that he was gathering fuel for the big fire.

Willow heard him, but couldn't interfere without drawing more attention to his blunder.

"What big fire?" Tall Reed demanded.

"For the feast," Thistle declared. Then, realizing his mistake, he babbled on with heightened spirit. "Thorn sees a feast coming. He knows what lies ahead. He will call the seals. The Boundless have power over them."

Willow and Crab exchanged glances of alarm. Thorn, finishing a loop on the side of the boat, hunched over his work as though he could shut himself away from Thistle's bragging.

Tall Reed walked up toward the hut cluster.

For a while everything seemed as before. Men were fashioning tree-boats and repairing old ones. Children were netting small fish. Women were pounding roots and chewing skins.

Still, by the time the sun was high the people were gathered along the shore to witness the calling of the seals. Thorn scanned this throng and declined to sing.

"You must," Crab said to him. He turned to Willow. "Tell him."

But Thorn wasn't the person Willow wanted to speak to.

She sought out Thistle, who was moving among the people, assuring them of the marvel to come.

"If you have nothing better to do," Willow said to him, keeping her voice low and neutral, "come with me now."

All eagerness and confidence, he obeyed. When they were out of earshot, she faced him, her eyes ablaze. She managed to keep her voice down. "Spoiler!" she hissed. "Thorn is not yours to boast of. Do you think that he performs for you?"

"He will. It is in our plan. That is why I have promised everyone—"

"Say no more. You make matters worse."

He stood up to her fury. "I have done no harm. Anyway, if Thorn cannot get away, he will be safe here. He is admired."

Was Thistle backing out? "Crab said you were with us," she whispered fiercely.

"I was. I am. If Thorn chooses a voyage in solitude, then I will help. Have helped."

Aghast, she realized that he understood nothing and no one, neither Thorn nor Crab nor herself. Did this make him more dangerous or less? How could she deal with him? Berating him only increased the chance that he might blurt out something damaging to their plan.

"Yes," she told Thistle. Seething, she managed to summon a conspiratorial tone. "You have helped. You will help. The time has come to ready ourselves, and that means you and Crab should stay close together. If matters change, our plans may shift. Afterward … afterward you will be free to say what you like."

The soft crooning of the seals floated on the quiet air. There were several voices at intervals. If Thorn was calling to them, she couldn't tell his song from theirs.

She and Thistle walked back to the beach, to all appearances on friendly terms. By the time they joined Crab at the boat, the seals were in retreat, their wet, brown eyes on the throng, the sleek heads sinking out of sight.

"Try calling some more," Crab urged Thorn.

But Thorn shook his head. "It is no good. I am no good. The seals know."

After the disappointed throng disbanded, Thorn quietly resumed his finishing touches on the boat. He acted as though his failure to summon the seals didn't matter. Meanwhile the men who had readied tree-boats for the seal kill were arguing about whether they should have attempted pursuit during their fleeting opportunity.

They were hauling up their tree-boats when Uncle Redstone shouted from the top of a dune and pointed seaward. Porpoises chasing prey headed straight for the shallows. At once the men launched their boats again and paddled out until they could swing around behind the porpoises. In the turmoil of the hunt, the water seemed to boil with diving and plunging beasts. Although one boat capsized, the others managed to drive two of the porpoises onto the beach.

After that the boat and its man were easily rescued. Everyone regrouped on the sand, elated over the catch and the easy slaughter.

"This is what I told you," Thistle exclaimed loudly. "There will be a feast. When Thorn called, the sea delivered this gift."

Willow said to Crab, "Take him somewhere. Keep him still."

"Keep him busy," said Thorn, laughing. "Far from here."

After the boys departed, Willow began to worry that Great

Mother might have miscalculated when she counted on the deep sleep that would follow the feast. With everyone intent on the taking of meat and slow to attend the fire, the night's brief darkness might come and go before the people lay senseless in their huts.

If only Crab would come back. Without Thistle. If only she could suggest to Tall Reed, without being obvious, that the children should start gathering dried kelp. If only she had remembered to ask Great Mother where, during her wandering, she had come upon shadow creatures like Thorn's.

Now it was too late. Great Mother had made clear that she should be left to herself until it was time to set off. She would appear at full dark, when she was certain all the people were in their huts sleeping off the feast. Only then would she climb into the boat, to be bundled out of sight, her every move as swift and silent as she could manage.

THORN

One of the women brought a huge portion to me. I wanted to share it with the dog, but he was skulking around with the rest of the pack, just near enough to snap up any scraps that dropped to the ground. I thought he might be parting from me already, letting me go.

I find it hard to do as much for him.

A man asked me why I was not eating. I said I was weary. I said I would eat after I slept. I wanted to make my own way, but he carried me and left me inside the bed closet. He stood watching me roll myself in the sealskin. I drew my head beneath the cover.

He waited awhile before rejoining the feast. I wondered how long I would have to remain like this, unmoving. After what seemed a long time someone entered the hut and paused near me. Cautiously I shifted so that part of my head could be seen. Whoever had come to check on me withdrew. The talk and laughter outside went on.

Then someone else came and spoke softly. "Thorn." It was Crab. "Quick," he whispered. "Straight to your corner in the work place. I brought your stick."

"Someone might see me," I whispered back.

"Willow is at the entrance. She is watching."

Crab took my place in the bed closet. "I had hoped to send you off," he said. "But we dared not put Thistle here. Journey well."

"Will there be trouble for you when they find you here?" I asked him.

"They will find no one. As soon as you are gone, Willow or Thistle will come for me."

There was no time for more. The deer bone sounded too loud tapping the stone floor, but I needed it to make haste. I caught a glimpse of Willow moving outside. I followed and turned in to the work place. A moment later she was at my side.

"We cannot stow the food and tools until everyone goes to sleep," she said. "When it is done, I will come for you. There is an extra oar. The boat is nearly afloat. The tide is rising. Once we are outside, no more talk."

"Who is with Thistle now?" I asked.

"No one. He began to eat just as the others were finishing. He may gorge himself."

"And then sleep?" I asked.

"Not if I get my hands on him," she answered.

We both smiled. Then she slipped away.

I was glad that she would be with Thistle to shove me off, for I still could not rid myself of the feeling that she sensed my intention to give myself to the sea. I did not believe she would thwart me. But in spite of her fervor in preparing the boat and arranging my escape, this one doubt remained smoldering like a live ember buried in ash, ready to burst into flame.

People began to straggle into their huts. If only darkness would come now. The moon shed so much light it left eerie shadows, even inside. Thinking of shadows, I glanced down to find my shadow figures still in place. I retrieved the fire stone from my pouch and added one final shape to those I had scratched upon the stone. I made the boat just as it is, with its basket shape and its buoyant bird stomachs and its wing of wings. I set it upon the shadow sea among the shadow seals. It is for Willow, to remove doubt, to help her believe in my purposeful journey.

As I was about to return the fire stone to my pouch, I stopped to consider one last time how I might leave it for her without arousing suspicion. Something so perfect should be passed from one person to another, not lost to the sea. But I did not want it to fall into the wrong hands or have Willow discover it with regret, thinking it left by chance. Would she think that? Could she believe that I might discard by chance my finest tool? Others might, but not Willow. The thought of chance could gain admittance only through some mighty rift. Even with all that remained unspoken between us, there was no rift.

When she came for me, I was still mulling over how to leave it so that she would understand it was meant for her. Then all consideration ended, and there was only action. She rushed ahead through the bright night, stopping often to let me catch up. She did not speak, although every gesture urged me to quicken my lopsided gait. Once I tumbled as I plunged from a grassy dune into a deep hollow. I rolled over and scrambled up as fast as I could.

Still silent, she waited, then moved on. Finally I looked ahead and saw the sea glinting black, as shiny as fire stone. There was the boat, there Thistle, stooping to hold it for me. It seemed to take a lifetime before I reached the water's edge.

Thistle said, "The balance …"

Willow hushed him. Not a word, she mouthed. We were done with speaking.

I stumbled over the steering oar and fell into the boat. I

noted as I righted myself that Thistle and Willow had rearranged the containers so that the large bundles were at the front. That must have been for balance, since I had to position myself at the rear to steer.

Noting all the care that had been taken to bring us to this moment, I knew I must guard against regret lest it eat away my resolve. Besides, there was no time now to wonder what might have been. Behind me Willow and Thistle lifted and shoved. Then they gave one final push, and at once the boat floated free.

The wing flapped until I grabbed a steering rope. Even if the fitful breeze had favored me, I could not rely on it. So I let the wing swing back and forth, seized the extra oar, and paddled with all my strength toward the open sea.

A smothered cry from shore made me glance back over my shoulder. I saw Willow splash into the shallows. Next I caught sight of what she pursued. The dog! He was swimming after me. If I kept on, so would he, until he could swim no more. I could not bear this. But if I stopped for him, if I tried to drag him into the boat, it would be swamped.

"Go back," I called to him. My voice set off an alarm among the roosting seabirds. Under cover of their babble, I called once more. "Go back!"

Just when I thought I must surrender to save him and give up all thought of escape, I saw a tree-boat head toward him, Willow and Thistle plying their oars on either side. As I stared, I could feel my boat beginning to wallow in the growing swells, and I realized I had let it swing sideways. So I paddled, too, reclaiming my course, heading straight for the horizon.

When I dared glance back again, I saw Willow stretched

full length on the tree-boat. She was reaching into the water. I paddled a few more strokes and looked once more. She and the dog were tangled together atop the tree-boat, and it was turning back.

I felt such a pang then. I had not thought it would be so hard to leave the dog and Willow and Crab and, yes, even Thistle. If only I could endure being captive to their people. At least for a while I have this boat, which was of their making as well as mine.

Farther out it began to lose way whenever it climbed a swell. It needed taming. Each time it slid down a trough of water, I paddled furiously to push it upward and on.

As soon as I cleared the headland, I took up a wing rope and hauled it toward me. How the boat sprang to life! It shuddered, as if to resist the wing's tug. I saw one bundle lurch as though alive, but it stayed in place, and I was free to attend to my seaward course.

The wing filled and stretched. It seemed determined to fly beyond my reach. Then it yielded and held to the crosswind. The stricken feathers made the sound of a bird in flight.

The boat soared!

WILLOW

Now. Now Great Mother is unwrapping herself. Now she is revealed to Thorn, who is astonished.

No, not now. Not yet.

I wait another moment. Now? There is Thorn, who believes he is alone in the boat. Here is Great Mother, glad to shift her aching body. But it is still too soon. So the moment passes, and I wait some more.

Finally I accept what I already know. Great Mother will remain hidden until Thorn ties the rope to himself and sleeps a little. That is when she will emerge.

Crab says, "Why do you stand there? They are gone."

"Yes," I reply, "gone. Flying over the water."

Glancing back at him, I notice a hint of first light on the inland horizon. It brings dim landshapes into sight. Yet the sea still holds darkness in its depths and in the sheltering sky.

Crab says, "After all the care we have taken, they will not turn to land until they are well away from here. You told Thistle and me that we are to know nothing about Thorn's flight. It is the same for you. When the uncles awaken, they should not find you looking out to sea."

He is right to prod me, to insist that I leave. And I am rigid with cold. Still, I feel rooted to the water's edge. No matter that the boat is out of sight. It tugs at my thoughts, so that I am scarcely here at all. I am with Thorn and Great Mother, feeling the ocean's pulse through oiled sealskin and bundled reeds, facing the unknown. Seeking a beginning place.

Crab says, "Soon it will be morning. We should sleep awhile."

When I fail to respond, he turns from me. He has been here since Thistle went to release him from Thorn's bed closet. Thistle did not return to the beach, but Crab came at once and has kept this vigil through the night. I know that I should follow him now to the huts.

But I enter the work place instead. The dog pads after me. Within the stone walls it is still too dark to see much. It doesn't matter, though. We know our way, the dog and I. Here is Thorn's corner. Great Mother's corner.

Shivering, I sink down onto a scrap of skin. The dog, still wet, stretches beside me. As I draw my knees up for warmth, something hard bites into my shoulder. I shift my weight to shove it aside. As soon as my fingers close around it, I know what I hold in my hand. It is the fire stone.

Thorn's voice comes at me, sharp and clear: "How would Willow use the fire stone, if I could leave it behind?"

I never did say how. I heard his question as a trap and set one for him instead. Yet it is here now, the fire stone. Thorn has given it in spite of my trickery.

This, then, is my answer: The fire stone will hasten the making of the next boat. A boat for seeking and finding. That is how I will put it to use. And then, if I can, I will bring it to you.

Such a promise! Great Mother would remind me that where bold thoughts leap up, deeds may yet falter. I do know that. What I cannot know is whether I am maker enough for what lies ahead. Even with the fire stone, even with Crab and Thistle alongside, the task will demand true craftiness, true care.

I draw close to the dog, seeking his wet warmth, his steadiness, his sense of Thorn. And I begin to believe. There will be another winged boat. Through rising mists of sleep, I can all but see it flying over the water.